A LOVE SONG FOR DREAMERS

RIVALS #3

PIPER LAWSON

Content editing by Becca Mysoor
Line and copy editing by Cassie Roberston and Joy Editing
Cover design by Lori Jackson
Cover photography by Regina Wamba

1

Annie

I've never watched a ballet with blood before.

But that's what this is.

The two EMTs move around Tyler in a dance they've rehearsed, one I've never seen and have no part in. He's strapped to a stretcher and lifted into the back of an ambulance. One of the techs, a woman, asks me questions about what happened.

I try to answer, but I can't take my eyes from Tyler—not when they put a mask over his face that hides his shallow breathing or when the lights inside the vehicle make his pale face look yellow. After the stretcher is locked in place in the ambulance, the vehicle takes off.

I want to hold him, but there's so much blood. It

covers his dark dress shirt, making it stick to his torso and his arm...

My stomach lurches.

They've got his shirtsleeve up and his arm lifted in the air.

I perch on a stool near Tyler's face, but his eyes are closed. I clutch my necklace hard enough my knuckles go numb, as if I can rewind time, can bring us back to the restaurant or the theater before a man I've never met ripped my reality in half.

"Hey, you," I murmur, brushing Tyler's damp hair away from his forehead. "It's going to be okay."

My heart's in my throat. I used to hate how it raced for him. Now I'd give it to him if it would bring color back to his pale face.

They hook him up to something, and a monitor beeps in slow intervals in the corner.

The vehicle bumps every now and again, and every time, the gurney jumps with it. I want to tell them this should be easier on him, but they're working away, one on each side, and the monitor continues to beep, and I can't even watch them.

In minutes or hours, the vehicle stops. The back doors swing wide, and a serious-looking man in scrubs eyes the scene inside the ambulance, his gaze finding me.

"Miss, you need to move out of the way."

I stumble out of the ambulance and watch them

lower Tyler to the ground, adjust the bed, and wheel him inside. I follow until they swing through a set of double doors, where I'm stopped by the same man from outside.

"I need to stay with him," I insist.

"Are you family?"

"He doesn't have anyone else."

His eyes soften. "Can you help with medical history?"

I follow him to chairs in the waiting room around the corner, answer his questions as best I can.

Still, I don't know if Tyler's parents or grandparents had heart disease. If he's ever had a reaction to medication.

What I do know is that he's strong and resilient and brave. That his smile fixes every problem I've ever known.

I know I love him and if he's not okay, I'm going to stop breathing.

Finally, the man sets down the clipboard. "Thank you. We'll let you know when we have more. If you need to leave, please see the administration desk first." He nods toward a window on one side of the room.

I pace the hallway. There are people in beds outside of rooms. *Is that what's going to happen to Tyler?*

I find my way to the desk. "I'm here with Tyler Adams. He's in the emergency room."

"I don't have any updates on Mr. Adams at this time."

"I know, but... he needs the best care available."

She pulls up a file on her computer. "Of course. All of our patients receive the best care our hospital can provide. Does he have insurance?"

My throat works. "I don't know. But it doesn't matter what it costs."

This shouldn't be happening. Everything was working out—with me, Tyler, our lives...

"Miss, are you feeling light-headed? You look pale."

"I'm fine." I force a smile and turn back down the hall, ignoring the people passing me.

I want to call my dad. He'd know what to do. More than that, I'd give anything to see him and Haley and Sophie brush through those doors.

A tear escapes down my cheek.

I open the contacts on my phone and hit his number. Each ring has my stomach twisting tighter, ready for the next second when he'll answer. I'll tell him I'm sorry for everything, that I'll make it up to him if only he'll help me with this one thing.

But there's nothing.

After four rings, I get his voicemail.

I try to formulate words to leave on a message.

Someone attacked Tyler with a knife.

He's bleeding like crazy.

We're at the hospital.

I don't know what the fuck to do.

It's all my fault.

A girl younger than me walks down the hall with a cast on her arm. Her parents are with her, but when she gets closer, I notice the scratches along her face, the bruises. She meets my gaze, and her face is composed.

Pull it together. For Tyler's sake.

The beep jerks me back, and I hang up without saying a word.

I swipe at my cheeks before making another call.

"Is he okay?" Beck demands as he stalks inside, Elle and Rae in tow. The clock on the wall says it's two in the morning.

I tell them what happened. As I'm finishing, a man in a suit enters the ER doors, searching the waiting room.

I rise to meet Zeke, the record exec who signed Tyler less than two weeks ago. "I told them to spare no expense, but..."

He understands immediately. "You don't think they'll take you seriously."

Zeke nods and goes to the desk, starts talking with the woman there.

"You called him?" Beck demands, coming up behind me.

"I need to know he's going to be taken care of. Zeke's interests and Tyler's are aligned. At least right now."

Rae strips off her sweatshirt and holds it out to me.

I stare at her, confused as to why she's offering me clothes when I have my own.

But when she keeps holding out the shirt, I look down at my dress and jacket, caked in blood.

When I start shaking instead of reaching for Rae's sweatshirt, Elle takes my hand and walks me to the bathroom. Rae's close on our heels.

Inside the clean six-stall ladies' room, I strip off my jacket and shove it in the garbage, revulsion taking over. Then I wash the blood off my hands, from under my fingernails.

The liquid soap doesn't do the best job, and I wish I had one of those bar soaps or an old toothbrush or something.

"It'll come out later." Rae's voice is calm, and it takes the edge off as I meet her steady gaze in the mirror.

I pull the sweatshirt over my dress, grateful it's at least hiding the blood.

Elle leans against one wall, looking paler than usual.

"You okay?" I ask her.

She lifts a shoulder. "My dad died in a hospital. It took a long time."

I hug her, for both of us, and she hugs me back.

Rae watches, and even though she's not part of this impromptu group hug, it feels like it. She's part of the moment, and their presence gives me strength.

When we get back outside, the waiting room includes Beck, a handful of strangers, and Zeke.

The ER doctor comes into the waiting room. "Miss Jamieson?"

But we're all on our feet as one while I say, "How is he?"

"He lost a significant amount of blood through a deep laceration in his forearm and hand. We've cleaned them, stitched them up. Not life-threatening. Your quick thinking helped keep it from getting there."

If it wasn't for me, he wouldn't have been there. We wouldn't have been walking home. If I hadn't worn his ring around my neck, hadn't made him fight for it, we would be back at his place right now.

"Miss Jamieson."

"What?" I blurt, shaking myself.

"Is Tyler right hand dominant?"

I nod.

"That should make recovery easier. He won't be doing anything with his left hand for some time."

A noise makes me realize I've dropped my bag on the floor.

Zeke answers for me. "The kid's a guitarist. He's going on tour in two weeks. He needs to play."

The doctor stares down the executive. "We've moved him to a private room. In time, he'll be able to look at options for reconstructive surgery. But playing guitar in two weeks is out of the question."

The reality of it settles around us, leaving the air heavy and cloying.

"Aside from pain," the doctor goes on, "there may be numbness in the arm and hand, limited to no mobility." My stomach sinks further. "But you can see him now, if you like."

"Yes." I look around at our friends, and they nod.

"You go," Beck says.

I follow the doctor down the hall and pause outside the room.

I listen through the door. There's the beeping of a machine. His heart rate.

No other sounds. No raging or groaning. Just silence.

I square my shoulders before heading inside. Tyler fills the bed with his broad frame, and it's shocking to see him so still. He's always full of life. Even when he's contained, there's a latent energy.

Tonight—this morning—there's nothing. And that terrifies me.

I stop beside the bed, peering down at his pale face. They've taken off the mask, and there are traces of lines on his face from where it sat. A thick white bandage covers from mid-forearm to his hand. His pale fingers stick out the end.

I lean over him. "Hey, handsome. How're you feeling?"

His eyes open half an inch, and his mouth moves a moment before producing a raspy sound. "Good as I look."

A breath whooshes out of me to hear him speak, as if I thought I might not again. "Beck and Elle and Rae are here. And Zeke. Do you need something else for the pain?"

Tyler shakes his head. "I can't feel my hand. It won't move. I can't..." His eyes close.

My gaze drags to his hand again. There's no hint of a rusty red stain through the white gauze, but my stomach turns anyway.

I can't imagine what he's going through. Not only physically, but the shock and hearing the doctor relay any part of what he told us.

The idea of him not being able to pick up his guitar tomorrow, to do what he's always done, washes over me in a wave of grief.

I want to hug him, or kiss him, or even cry.

Instead, I force myself to be strong for him. For us.

"I'm glad you're okay. You're going to be okay," I amend. I start to reach for his good hand, then see a spot of blood I missed on my wrist and tug Rae's sweater down to hide it.

"Am I?"

He says it so quietly I almost miss it.

2

Tyler

When my eyes crack open, the world is black and empty.

Maybe I'm not awake after all. Maybe I'm dead.

But as I turn my head, something cool and soft glides across my cheek. Satiny sheets. They're over me and under me, and my head is cushioned by a fat, fluffy pillow.

The green numbers on the digital clock next to my bed read 11:51.

I've woken up plenty and not known where I was, but as the hotel room comes back to me, I realize I've done it two mornings in a row. The blackness from the heavy curtains doesn't help.

My arm is numb. It's an improvement over the first time I woke up this morning, when it felt as if each muscle was being peeled from my fingers to my elbow.

Once when I was a kid, a brick from a construction site my friends and I were screwing around at fell on my hand from a stack a few feet high.

I couldn't feel my fingers for a couple hours. It sucked.

I'd give anything for that feeling now. What I have instead alternates between pain and numbness. Hell's see-saw.

I shift out of bed, the rest of my muscles aching. I can't shower because of the bandages, but I drag my body to the en-suite bathroom to take a bath.

When the doctor told me what happened two nights ago, the mess of painkillers kept me in a dizzy state of denial.

Lacerations. Severed tendons. Long-term damage.

All of it means I can't play guitar.

The emotions blur together like the sensations. There's panic, clawing at my throat. Disbelief, hammering in my head. And underneath it all, a grief I can't look at too closely yet because it means something I'm not ready to accept...

That no matter how long I sleep, in no world will I wake up and have everything be okay.

When I get out of the bath, I go to the drawer of clothes Beck brought over yesterday from our apartment. I grab boxer briefs and sweatpants and tug them on before heading out to the living room of the hotel suite. The smell of coffee is a small mercy, as is the shape of the girl in the kitchenette.

"You're back," I croak.

Annie turns and smiles, and the awful knot in my chest loosens a bit. "I went to class and picked up some supplies. Saw the nurse was here to change your bandage while I was gone."

I glance toward the table where a note the nurse left says just that. Without asking, Zeke hired her to check on me once a day in the hotel room he insisted on paying for "as long as I need."

The fact that he's keeping such a close eye is unsettling, but calling Zeke to demand why he's still treating me like an investment given how far my stock has plummeted in the last two days feels low on my priority list.

Annie looks at home in tight jeans and bare feet, a sweater zipped up over her tank top because I cranked the air conditioning. Her hair is twisted up in a knot on her head, Annie's method of keeping it out of her way when she's got bigger things to worry about.

She crosses to me, searching my face for signs of... I don't know. Trauma. Depression. General fucked-up-ness.

I wish she'd stop.

"Nurse wanted to give me a sponge bath too." I try for a joke.

Annie's gaze drags down my bare chest to where my sweatpants hang low on my hips.

"I told you I'd change the bandages for you." There's concern in her voice but also a note of something that makes my dick twitch.

"Nah. Then my girlfriend wouldn't get all jealous."

"Do I look jealous?" She tilts her head, lips curving.

"Yeah. You do." I reach for her with my good hand. It still takes conscious effort not to move the other one, but I grab her waist and tug her against me.

Her cool palms flatten against my chest. She's a reminder not everything in this world is upside down.

Annie tips her face up for a kiss, but I turn away at the last second. "Ah. Forgot to brush my teeth. Be right back."

I head into the bathroom and reach for my toothbrush.

Last night was my first full night out of the hospital, and Annie refused to sleep next to me, afraid to risk grabbing my arm.

But she wouldn't sleep at the dorms, either,

instead opting for the pull-out couch in my hotel room.

She's been glued to my side since I got out of the hospital, but I haven't told her everything.

Like the fact that I can't stop thinking about that night.

It happened so fast, but when I replay it, it's slow. All the things I could've done. Should've done.

All the different ways we could've gotten home.

Shoving it away doesn't work, so I've tried starting the memory earlier, at the musical I took her to or in the bar when I gave her that ring.

The problem is it feels as if those memories are getting fuzzier and further away and the ones in the dark alley are getting sharper and closer.

A knock on the suite door outside as I finish brushing my teeth has my ears perking up.

"I'm here with reinforcements." Beck's cheerful voice echoes from the other room, and I step toward the barely open bathroom door to listen. "Male strippers."

Annie laughs, the first time I've heard her laugh since the hospital. It makes my chest hurt.

"How is he?"

"The pain seems more manageable."

"That's not what I mean."

She doesn't answer.

"I can hear you," I taunt as I head back in to find Beck seated on the couch.

"Dammit. Even the part where I made out with your girl?"

I narrow my gaze on him. "Try it and you'll lose more than a hand."

He chuckles. "I talked to your profs about getting extensions on your term projects." He runs me through the list of accommodations they've made for me. "Even printed out your study notes for finals."

"Thanks," I say, and mean it. "I'll get to it eventually."

I rise and go to the kitchen, where Annie's looking over her shoulder at me.

"You don't want to take a look today?" she says. "You must be getting sick of watching Netflix."

"Doesn't seem so urgent." I survey the bowl of marshmallows and box of Rice Krispies cereal someone must've brought, because I'm pretty sure they weren't in the hotel cupboards.

"This, though—this is a priority." She smiles. "Here, lemme help."

I take the bowl and stick the marshmallows and butter in the microwave. When I grab a spatula and turn, I bump into her, jostling my arm. I hiss out a breath of pain.

"Shit. I'm sorry," she murmurs. "You should sit down."

"I can microwave marshmallows."

"Evidently you can't, bro," Beck calls.

Every muscle in my torso tightens, but I grab my coffee and sink into the chair across from Beck.

I watch Annie make the squares as Beck catches me up on stuff from school.

"This is a nice place," he says after a few minutes. "Zeke's taking care of you."

Annie comes over and sets a plate of squares on the table. "He knows you're going to recover. There are options for reconstruction. The doctor said so himself, and physio—"

"Physio won't do shit when what's in my hand is sliced in two," I state.

Annie and Beck are quiet while I take a bite of a square. It tastes familiar, but everything else has changed.

"You're still a musician," Annie says. "This doesn't change that. Zeke believes in you."

"He gets a paycheck when people bring in money, which I don't see me doing. He has a tour leaving in ten days, and if I can't play, there's no way the invite still stands."

My voice has a new edge. The anger's not directed at Annie, but she stiffens.

Beck looks between us before rising from his seat. "I'll leave you guys to it. One for the road?"

I don't say anything as Beck takes a treat and

leaves.

Once the door's closed, I shove out of the chair and say what we're both thinking.

"I'm sorry. I'm being an asshole."

I drop onto the couch, and Annie shifts onto the arm, tucking her feet up in front of her as she watches me.

"It's understandable," she says softly.

"It's not. None of this is understandable."

A wave of panic rises up, and I fight to keep it down. It's a losing battle.

I've never felt out of control. No one has ever made me out of control. They can take things from me—home, family. I'll survive. But this…

I've always managed myself. I'm the one I can count on. But now I'm broken. Someone took *me* from me.

The worst part is I never saw it coming. I was prepared to lose everything, had felt that before between walking away from Annie and then having my dad die in front of me and losing my contract after.

But how can you prepare for the possibility of losing *yourself*?

The question is still spinning in my mind when Annie shifts over me, careful not to bump my bandaged arm. Her weight settles across my thighs, and suddenly my attention's on her, not my fucked-up life, not my fucked-up hand. It's impossible to think of anything but her floral scent and the way she feels pressing against my groin.

My bad arm's off to the side as if I can forget it by keeping it out of sight. With my good hand, I brush the hair back from her earnest face, tuck it behind her ear.

No matter what's going on, I have this girl. It feels like a small mercy, but I know it's more than that. It's everything.

"Don't give up on me," I murmur.

Her eyes turn liquid. "Never."

Her lips find my neck, and I shift, giving her better access.

Maybe if I pretend hard enough to be normal, it'll happen.

"Back when we were kids," I start, "I used to check you out. I didn't admit it to myself. I'd tell myself I was curious what you'd come up with next, but I really wanted to stare at those lips. I was obsessed."

"Can I tell you a secret?" she murmurs, kissing down my chest. "They're obsessed with you, too."

My heart kicks. So does something else, because she's squirming in my lap. There's no hiding how hard I'm getting under my sweatpants.

"You're gonna kill me," I murmur at the ceiling as my head falls back on the couch. Cool air flows around my groin, and before I know it, a smooth hand fists my cock.

"You seem healthy to me," she replies.

My tortured groan ends on a laugh. "Annie—"

"Relax. You're supposed to be healing."

She works the pants down my hips, and I lift to help as my cock springs out.

The first stroke of her hand from tip to hilt has me hissing out a breath.

Fuck, yeah.

The second has my ass tightening, my hips thrusting up into her grip. Sharp pangs of pleasure jolt up my spine, pulling my balls tight. The blood flows through my veins, and I'm throbbing.

My arm throbs too.

It's been days since we've done this, and I haven't forgotten the need I have for her.

She's eager and open. She meets my gaze with a look of wickedness, silently telling me exactly what she's going to do next.

Yes.

This beautiful girl with a heart the size of the world is going to make me see stars.

But I can't kick the throbbing down the left side of my body.

Her tongue finds the head of my cock, licking the bead at the end, and that's what I need to forget everything.

I want to flip her over and drive into her until I'm so deep she'll never get me out. I want to spread her wide and eat her until the only word she knows is my name.

I can't.

So, I let her fuck me.

"Harder," I grunt.

She resists, licking down the underside of my dick while giving me a little squeeze at the bottom.

"You're saying you don't like this?" she teases before pulling my head into her mouth and sucking slowly.

I groan. "Annie." There's arousal in my voice, but the frustration has her brows pulling together. "Quit dicking around."

With a moment's hesitation, she moves back down my body and there's no dicking around this time. She fists me with both hands and takes me as far down as she can.

Yes. This is what I need.

I need her.

I need this moment. Everything's okay in this moment.

I catch her hair in my hand, twist it behind her head to keep it out of her way—and to tug on her, to pretend I'm dragging her toward the inevitable conclusion of this when she's the one dragging me.

A piece falls back in her face, and I capture it,

tugging it into the makeshift ponytail. Doing that jerks the necklace out from under her shirt.

The rose and the ring.

My heart twists.

I'm so close to coming, and the blood rushes in my veins as thoughts rush to the surface of my mind. They're incongruent, but they *feel* true.

I wish she'd never kept that rose.

I wish I'd put that ring on her finger.

I wish I hadn't stayed with my dad in the hospital and bailed on my first contract.

I wish I'd made us take a cab home.

I wish I'd never let her talk me into believing I could be more than I am.

When I come, she takes everything—my release and my anger and my devastation.

As I sag back into the cushions, Annie settles herself on my thighs once again. She kisses me, and I taste my own salt mixed with her.

"How does it feel now?" she asks, pulling back.

It sounds like a casual question, but it's not. She needs to make me whole again. It might as well be scrawled on her cheek, words she wrote herself.

"Better," I lie.

It's the one gift I can give her, and we've lost enough this week.

3

Annie

"Tell me why you want this job busting your ass for people who couldn't care less if you were born unless you forget the refill on their Pellegrino."

Beck's rapid-fire question has me leaning across the kitchen table in his and Tyler's apartment.

The first of my two final exams isn't until tomorrow, but already, I feel as if I'm being grilled.

"Because I need money to pay next semester's tuition and living expenses and my rock star dad cut me off for failing to tell him I was at performing arts school."

He cocks his head. "Cute. One more time."

I square my shoulders. "Because I'm a hard worker, I don't give up, and I'll wait whichever tables you tell me to for as many hours as you want."

"Good." Beck rises from his chair and goes to the fridge, where he pulls out two Coke cans and hands me one.

I pop the tab and take a long drink. "Thanks for helping me practice for interviews."

The reality that I need to provide for myself is sinking in. I've submitted resumes to at least twenty places—a few administrative positions, plus serving since there seem to be more of those available.

"Give them the answers they want, and someone will give you a chance."

My gaze scans the apartment, landing on the guitar leaning against the wall. "Think I should take his guitar to him at the hotel?"

"So he can play it with his teeth?" Beck's laughter dies when he sees my expression. "Manatee, he'll ask for it if he wants it."

That statement bothers me. Tyler's been doing his best to assure me he's okay, but it doesn't feel right.

"I ran into the nurse on my way to school this morning. She said his hand seems to be healing, but I don't know about the rest of him. Have you noticed anything strange in the last couple of days?"

The way Beck shifts against the counter, frowning, doesn't ease my mind.

I turn my soda can in my hands. "I know it'll take

time, and this is part of the process. He's been through a traumatic event, and—"

"You both have." Beck crosses the distance between us, tilting his face down to search my expression. "Tyler dropped one of his classes rather than rescheduling the final."

My brows shoot up. "What?" He didn't say anything this morning in the hour it took me to get up, shower, put away the pullout couch and leave for Vanier.

Beck shrugs. "I think he figured he had enough on his plate. The pain's been bad again."

Something else he didn't tell me. My hand tightens on the can until it makes a crunching noise, and I set it on the counter.

Beck lays a hand on my shoulder. "He's gonna work it out. It'll take time. More than four days."

But I hate the thought of Tyler lying to me. If he wanted to keep me from worrying, it's having the opposite effect.

I get why he kept things from me back in high school, when he was trying not to want me.

Now, we're together. We don't need secrets. They'll only keep us apart.

The door opens, and Tyler starts inside before pulling up, looking between Beck and me. "Hey. What are you doing here? I thought you were studying."

Beck's hand slides off my shoulder.

"Beck's helping me with practice interviews for jobs," I respond. "I'm surprised you're here."

"Needed some more clothes."

He hasn't been back since that night.

This is good. A step forward.

"Let me help." I follow him into his room. "Beck said you dropped a class."

"You're talking to Beck about me?" Tyler turns, arching a dark brow.

Before I can answer, Tyler closes the distance between us and presses me up against the door.

The expression on his face turns hungry in a heartbeat. He drops his mouth to mine, kissing me hard. There's an edge that didn't used to be there, as if he's proving a point. To me or himself, I don't know.

"We should talk," I protest even though my body's already loving his new plan.

"You don't want me." He says it like a statement, not a question, but when he pulls back to study me with dark eyes, there's a wariness underneath.

I take his face in my hands, struggling between giving into his immediate intention and forcing us to talk. About school, or what's in his head, or what I can do to help erase the dark shadows under his eyes.

Tyler's said himself he's a doer, not a talker. Besides, the fact that he showed up here is progress.

I can try to understand that instead of getting hung up on the fact that he's not telling me every thought in his head.

I can meet him where he is, get him through this however he needs.

"I always want you."

I wrap my arms around his neck and kiss him back. He reaches under my skirt to grab my tights, and I take over, working them down my legs. When I have one foot off, he pushes my hand back against the door and grinds into me.

I work on his jeans, get them and his boxer briefs down. He's positioned himself between my thighs, his mouth hungry on my jaw, my neck. I shut my eyes as my head falls back against the door, but we can't get the right angle.

"Bed," I murmur, and he tugs me toward it.

He drops down first, and I move over him. If this is what he needs, what we need, I can do it. Having tons of sex with my crazy-hot boyfriend is not a hardship.

He's breathing shallowly, eyelids at half-mast and gaze smoldering. "Feels like you're doing all the work lately, Six."

"If this is work, sign me up for overtime."

His shirt is halfway up his chest, revealing cut abs

and smooth skin I want to trace with my lips and tongue.

His slow smile grips my heart. "I owe you one. When this is all over, I am going to lie you down on this bed and eat you until you scream."

"Deal."

If I wasn't already wet, I'm soaked now.

I position him at my entrance, brushing him through my slickness once before I sink down on his cock.

We both groan at the feel of it, and I move to thread my fingers through his, hitching a breath when I realize I can only grab one.

His fingers tangle with mine, gripping hard, and I arch my back to take him as deep as he can go.

His heavy exhale is satisfying, but the look in his eyes isn't.

He's not here.

And it hurts.

I thought I could reach him without words, meet him the way that he understands.

But if he's not here when he's inside me, I don't know where to find him.

I don't know how to bring him back.

"Happy start of exams," Pen singsongs as she grabs my waist.

I lose my balance and wobble on the skates. "Only you would get excited at the prospect of high stakes written evaluation," I say once I right myself. "I only have two, but I might not survive it if you take me out and I end up concussed. I have a very high center of gravity."

"Hope you're talking about your huge brain... because your tits aren't that big."

I laugh, the cold air rushing down my throat.

The ice rink in Central Park is full on a weekday afternoon. Elle, Rae and I decided to take a break from cramming for finals in the Vanier library to meet up with Pen. It feels like a spot of brightness in the horror of the past week.

"Your parents must be stoked you're going home," I comment.

"My dad's been asking for weeks what food I want for the holidays. Knowing my mom, she's probably making it in small quantities so I don't get fat. Have you talked to your dad?" Pen prompts.

"No." I think of the unanswered call I made from the hospital a week ago. "But Haley sent me an 'exam emergency kit', with socks and notebooks and a huge Starbucks card. At least she's in my corner."

Pen's brows rise. "Did you tell her about Tyler?"

I stare past her at the dozens of people skating

happily around the rink oblivious to what's going on with us. "Not yet."

Pen slides to a crisp stop thanks to the figure skating lessons she took freshman year of high school. "How is he?"

"The wound is healing. But the cut only tells half the story. I found a list of the best physical therapists in New York, but Tyler says he can't afford them. I told him that's the only way he'll be able to play again, but he shut down."

Motion catches my eye, and I see Elle waving from the boards with cups of something on the railing in front of her. Rae's there too. I head for them, Pen gliding smoothly beside me as we weave through the skaters.

"I'm on to desperate measures—having sex just to get him to talk to me."

"We're talking about sex now? I would've put Baileys in this hot chocolate," Elle comments as we pull up next to the boards. Rae hands me a steaming cup.

I'm relieved to see them. Their comfort has been steadying. If there's a silver lining to what happened, it's that I have real friends here to support me. Not only that, but they understand the pressure Tyler's facing, because they signed up for it, too.

"Right now, it's the only time I feel connected to him. Tyler's never been the most talkative person, but… he used to talk to me. I think he talks to Beck. But I can't help feeling like he's slipping away. When we're together, I don't know if he's lying there thinking 'I'm lucky I'm not dead,' or 'I can't believe this happened to me,' or"—I take a breath—"'There goes my future.' I keep thinking it could have been worse. I could have lost him. But in a way, it feels like I already have."

It's the first time I've said those words out loud, and they gut me. The idea that he might not come back the same from this is horrifying.

It also feels selfish. How could he be the same? Tyler will have to live with the physical consequences of that night. Even if, through some miracle, they can repair his hand and he can play the way he used to, it'll be a long road back.

Two empathetic faces peer back at me from under knit hats, Pen's from between her earmuffs.

"He loves you. That much hasn't changed, and no one can take that away," Pen reassures me.

When Pen heads for the benches to take off her skates, chatting with Elle as she goes, Rae stays behind, pulling something out of her jacket pocket.

"I got this for you."

She holds up a little souvenir Statue of Liberty figurine on a short chain.

I take in Lady Liberty's resolute expression. "Is this a reminder I'll always be a tourist?"

"No. It's a reminder that New York welcomes people, even if it doesn't always feel that way. And that grace and strength aren't opposites. Sometimes, having both is the only way to survive."

Touched, I take the tiny figure and throw my arms around Rae before she can protest.

"Thank you."

"It's not a big deal," she mumbles back, squirming. "It was five dollars."

I think about the way Tyler acted after the showcase. He went inside himself and came out with the performance Beck recorded that ended up scoring him the contract with Zeke.

Maybe he needs a reminder of who he is, what he does.

"You guys want to go to Leo's tonight? I know we're all studying, but only for an hour. Two, tops," I ask as we catch up to Elle and Pen by the bench.

Elle cocks her head, intrigued. "You have something special lined up?"

"Not yet." Conviction surges through me. "But I will."

"You came!" Elle calls from where she's perched next to Beck on a stool at Leo's.

She hugs Tyler, and he wraps his good arm around her for a second.

"I heard that due to your condition, you got an extension until January to write your exams," Elle says.

"The gifts never end," he drawls, but his mouth lifts at the corner when he looks back at me, and my heart lifts with it.

It's not the only reason to be in a good mood. I emerged from the library after skating to find two calls about interviews for serving jobs. Plus, I've started investigating both student loans and scholarships to help cover tuition and living expenses next semester.

Rae orders drinks for the crew—alcohol for all of us except Tyler, who's still on medication and gets a Coke—and we catch up through a few of the open mic acts.

Some Vanier students stop by to talk, and the tightness in my chest eases every time Tyler lets them draw him into conversation. I'm thrilled to see him talking and laughing with our friends.

Beck said Tyler would need time, and he was right.

I catch Beck's eye and he lifts his glass almost imperceptibly. I smile, sighing out a big breath I've been holding for ages.

It almost feels like old times.

Almost.

"Come on, I have a surprise for you." Excitement bubbles through me as I take Tyler's good hand and lead him backstage.

"A surprise. Are we going to have sex backstage?"

"Better."

"No such thing."

I nod to the woman who does the bookings, and she smiles.

"Heard you had a little setback," she calls to Tyler. "Nice to see you back in action."

"You call this action?" he tosses, lifting his arm.

"Chicks dig scars."

The current performer finishes, and I jerk my head toward the stage. "Let's go."

He balks. "Go where?"

I head out to the stage and pull a guitar over my head, nodding to the other mic. A cheer goes up—not for me but from the people who spot Tyler in the wings.

I lean into the mic. "So, this is the performance that's been delayed a few weeks. But it's the one we planned."

I play the first few chords of our showcase song, and a new round of hoots goes up.

Tyler doesn't move.

I step back from the mic, continuing to play as I

cross to him in the shadowy wings. "Come on! I've never had to drag you onto a stage before."

But whatever's going on behind those shuttered eyes is dark and private.

"You want me to sing," he says at last.

"Yes. You sang at the showcase. You were amazing."

His expression grows darker. "I'm not a singer, Annie. I'm a guitarist. So, give me the damn guitar."

My fingers still on it. "What?"

"You heard me."

I lift it over my head.

The crowd's gone silent.

He takes it with his good hand, shifts it over his head. He tries to hold the strings with his bandaged hand, his face contorting from the effort or the result.

I suck in a breath. Tyler's pain is mine, and it's awful. "It'll take time—"

"It'll take a fucking miracle."

He shoves the guitar into my arms and walks off stage.

I chase him into the wings, grabbing his shoulder to make him turn back.

"All I wanted was to be a studio musician, Six. I didn't used to believe in dreams, but you made me. And I wish to hell you hadn't."

It could be worse.

That's my mantra right now as I curl up in the stacks of the library at Vanier studying.

Yes, my boyfriend got stabbed and he hates music, and maybe me. After last night at Leo's, he went back to his hotel and I didn't follow him, staying in my dorm room for the first time in over a week.

But hey. I survived my first exam this morning and in another forty-eight hours, I can apply myself with renewed energy to the cause of finding money to stay in school.

I'm setting down the notes for my Entertainment Management exam tomorrow when my phone vibrates in my bag.

The number has me stiffening.

"Hello," I answer under my breath.

"Hi." My dad's voice is rough. "You called."

"Nine days ago."

I pack up my things and head outside so I don't disturb the other students taking up study cubes and lounging in comfy chairs.

There are a few students out here, too, but not any close enough to listen, if they'd even care. The hype around my dad has all but evaporated. Something else to be grateful for.

He huffs out a breath. "I needed time to think about what happened. Haley said I might have overreacted in New York."

"You think?"

My voice is sharp enough a girl halfway down the hall lifts her head, and I turn away.

"You lied to me, Annie. To both of us." I can hear him trying to get control of himself.

But as I lean against a wall, I can't bring myself to care.

"Tyler got hurt. We were walking home at night. Someone jumped him." I take a breath. "He's going to be okay."

"Jesus. Annie, what about you?"

"I'm taking care of him."

"That's not what I meant." He curses. "Come home. We'll deal with all of this once you're back."

I want to. If he'd answered last week when I called and told me he'd fix it all, I would've taken him up on it in a heartbeat.

My fingers find the little Statue of Liberty keychain and I turn it in my hand.

"You told me life in this industry never goes the way you plan, and you're right. I came to New York to pursue my dreams. You may not agree with them, but you don't have to. I'm not giving up."

I think he's going to argue, but he doesn't.

"Haley and I will pay your tuition if that's what you want."

My chest expands in relief. *I don't need to get a job,*

don't need to struggle to figure out how I'm going to stay here.

But my gaze plays over the students in the hall. They're from all walks of life, all of them here because they can't imagine being anywhere else. What they all have in common is they're here on their terms.

The realization that hits me is sobering and freeing at once.

"You taught me how to swim. You taught me how to love music. But there's one thing you taught me without meaning to, and it's how to make it without giving a fuck what anyone thinks. I don't need your approval or your money. You started out in this industry when you were my age, and you made it on your own. I will too."

There's silence on the line, punctuated only by hoarse breathing.

"When are your exams finished?" he asks at last.

"Next week."

"Come home. Bring Tyler."

I run a finger over the ridges of the tiny figurine's torch, her gown, her pedestal. "I am home, Dad."

4

Annie

"There's a problem with your writing," Ms. Talbot informs me, looking up from the computer in her office.

It's quiet at Vanier since exams finished yesterday. Only a handful of students staying for the holidays remain, plus a number of the faculty.

"What's that?" I ask.

"It's better than any other student's I've seen. These lyrics you wrote are meaningful and specific."

My shoulders relax. I didn't realize how much tension I was holding until she said those words. "Thank you."

"I'd like you to help me finish the book for this show. It doesn't pay much, but it's a good learning experience. And you should consider auditioning, at the right time."

Excitement surges through me. "I'd love to."

I could be in an off-Broadway show. One I helped write.

"But," she goes on, "I need your commitment. You pulling out of the showcase was shortsighted and foolish."

"I understand. This is my dream. I'll do whatever it takes to see it through."

"Good." Her gaze narrows. "On another front, I heard about Mr. Adams' injury. I'm sorry. He was a tremendous talent."

"Is," I correct. "He can't play yet. But he's still the same person he was."

In the days since Leo's, I haven't slept at Tyler's hotel.

I wanted to help him. Wanted him to open up.

He did, didn't he?

He said he wished I hadn't made him believe in something bigger.

"Life changes us." Talbot's voice brings me back. "It can happen over years or in an instant. He may never be the same person. But there's another risk, which is that you might lose yourself in trying to find him."

I want to reject her words, but my throat is too tight to produce sound.

"How old are you?" she goes on.

"Nineteen."

Her clear eyes crease at the corners. "Life will change you in more ways than you can imagine, good and bad. Now, you have an opportunity. Don't let that go to waste."

I nod. "Thank you, Ms. Talbot."

"Annie."

I don't realize the tear has streaked down my cheek until she holds out the tissue.

"Call me Miranda."

On my way out, I make a decision.

Tyler and I need to talk. Maybe he's wrong and maybe I am, but we're going to figure this out together.

The whole subway ride over to Tyler's hotel, I'm torn between thoughts of him and the opportunity I've been given.

When I get up to street level at the other end of the line, there's an incoming call on my phone.

"Miss Jamieson, this is the financial aid office at Vanier. I know the last time we spoke there wasn't anything available, but we have new funding that hadn't been added to our online system. It would cover tuition, plus a stipend."

I pull up in the middle of the street, the backs of my eyes burning.

"Miss Jamieson? Are you still there?"

"Yes, I'm still here." I swallow.

I could stay in school and have this huge opportunity.

"Are you interested in applying?"

"Yes. Yes, of course. Thank you."

After hanging up, I bound to Tyler's hotel.

When I get to his suite, he's gone. But a note scrawled on the hotel stationary on the counter says he went to a meeting at the studio.

I hope they're not kicking him out.

Although, maybe it would be for the best if he went back to his apartment. He needs to get back into his routine, his life.

If this is your last time here, you might as well take advantage.

I write a note back to Tyler, then put on my bathing suit, which I'd brought over last week and hadn't had a chance to use, and head down the elevator.

The swimming and fitness area is quiet midafternoon. As I dive in the deep end, the feel of the water on my body is heaven. I front crawl the length of the space, then back. Again.

I put in a dozen laps, then another dozen, until my muscles burn and my head is clear.

When I finally lift my head and take off my goggles, pulling myself up with my forearms to rest on the edge of the pool, a pair of shoes fills my vision. I peer up those denim-clad legs, the dress shirt, the towel under one arm.

There will never be a day when seeing Tyler Adams doesn't make me happy.

"Hi," I say, smiling. "How was your meeting?"

"Surprising." He drops the towel on the deck and crouches down.

I notice a slip of paper in his hands. "Are they kicking you out of the hotel? We knew it'd happen eventually. I can help you move your stuff home."

I shift forward to take the paper, my damp fingers leaving drops on its surface.

"It's a first-class ticket to London. Leaving tomorrow." My brain struggles to do the math. When I put the pieces together, they leave me breathless. "He still wants you on the tour."

Tyler grimaces. "I can't play guitar worth shit. But he wants to capitalize on my fifteen minutes of fame after the video from Beck's vlog as the frontman of some manufactured band."

"By performing music," I emphasize. "This is a good thing."

He turns away.

I set the ticket carefully on a dry part of the deck before hoisting myself out. I wrap the towel around myself as I straighten, grabbing the ticket again. I follow him as he paces the length of the pool.

"So, you're okay with it?" he tosses over a shoulder. "You want me to live out of busses and planes with a bunch of dudes. To flirt with women who think more about what it'd be like to fuck me than the music I'm making."

Jealousy rises up, and I shove it back down. "That's not what this is."

If he goes on tour, it won't matter if he plays guitar or sings or juggles on stage with his feet. He'll make it work. The audience will love him because his intensity, his seriousness, his capability, will shine through.

He pulls up, still facing away. "With a guitar in my hands, I'm better than anyone at Vanier. Better than Jax. Or I was—two weeks ago. They took it from me."

The rawness in his voice guts me. I move in front of him, cupping his face and forcing him to look at me with angry eyes. "No one can make you less than you are. And there are plenty of ways to make music, Tyler."

But his cynical expression makes me sick.

Talbot's words come back to me. *Am I the one who's deluded?*

These last two weeks have been a nightmare.

His hand is healing, but the rest of him is dying.

I've tried everything to pull him out of it, to show him I'm here for him and we'll get through this together.

He still tells me he loves me, but if he turns down

this tour and moves out of the hotel, is this what our new normal will be? His bitter accusations? Me walking on eggshells?

The other night at Leo's, the way he looked at me and at the guitar... That was not the man I love. If he doesn't love music, I don't know who he is.

I press the ticket against Tyler's chest, my eyes burning. "You should do it."

"What?"

For the first time, the anger leaves his face and he's my Tyler again. The curious, thoughtful boy with the fast hands and the slow smile.

He looks past me, watching a family emerge from the changing room to get into the pool behind us.

"You made me promise once to never leave you."

"I'm asking you to."

The words hang between us.

My hands fist at my sides hard enough my nails dig into my palms. "Miranda—Talbot," I go on at his confusion, "wants my help with the musical. She says I should audition when it's finished."

Tyler reaches up to tug on his hair. "Wow. Congrats. Your dreams are coming true when mine are going up in smoke."

"I know you're going through something unimaginable, but don't accuse me of holding my success over you."

His gaze works over mine as if he's trying to see through my words, trying to understand.

"I didn't mean it like that," he says at last, gesturing toward the doors. "We should go upstairs."

We head up to his room, and I shower quickly and throw my clothes back on.

He doesn't try to join me.

If I expected the tension to have dissipated by the time I'm back in the living area, it hasn't.

Tyler's standing by the window. He cuts a look toward me when I emerge. "If I go on tour, what happens?"

"You get to light up a stage."

"I meant to us."

I count the beats of my heart, the slow, steady rhythm reminding me the world is still turning, even though it feels as if everything's stopped.

I reach for the necklace I put back on after the swim, but it feels too much like a tell. So, I force my hand down to my side as I cross to him at the window, my gaze lingering on the ticket on the coffee table as I pass it.

When I stop in front of him, he hooks a finger in my belt loop to fit my hips to his. That tiny gesture nearly breaks me, and when I look up to see Tyler's handsome face full of frustration and confusion, that only makes it harder.

Miranda's words come back to me. There's so

much ahead for both of us. We've always been striving toward greatness, no matter how far away it feels and no matter what gets in the way.

I want this chance for Tyler.

I want it for me, too.

"I know this isn't what you wanted," I start, "but it's still an opportunity. And even if it doesn't feel like it right now, you will hate yourself if you don't try."

I will hate myself if I let you quit trying.

The tears are threatening to spill over. For once, I shove the emotions down.

Instead, I kiss him. It's deep and hard, and every second that my lips move over his, I'm fighting the burning behind my eyes with everything in me.

When he pulls back, my panicked thought is that it's too soon. I need more of him, need his lips on me and his comfort in me, and even if he's not quite my Tyler, he's here and that's enough.

"I'll go."

His words make my stomach drop. The relief I was expecting never comes, but I nod anyway.

"It'll be good," I promise. I press up on my toes to wrap my arms around him in a fierce hug. "I'm so proud of you. Call me from London, okay? I don't care what time you get in."

Tyler exhales hard, and when I force myself to pull back, the beautiful gaze I know better than my own moves between my lips and my eyes.

"Six...Why does this feel like goodbye?"

The nickname makes my heart swell and shatter at once.

I force my mouth to smile, and every muscle hurts. "It's not."

But I know the truth.

Deep down, I know it is goodbye.

5

———

Annie

TWO AND A HALF YEARS LATER

"Why is it always prodigal sons and never prodigal daughters?" Elle's voice comes over the phone as I shift into the limo outside the terminal at DFW.

"Maybe women are smart enough not to go back."

"Or they didn't leave it so long in the first place."

As the car pulls away, I slide my sunglasses up my nose. "Going home might be the worst idea you've had since becoming my roommate."

"It wasn't my idea. Haley invited you on behalf of her and your dad. I just played the dead dad card and reminded you that it sucks not to have a dad in the first place."

"You're right. And I'll be back in New York first thing Monday. You won't even notice I'm gone," I say as we wind our way through the mass of ramps and overpasses.

"Well, someone noticed. He's been knocking on the door again."

Just what I need. "I'll handle him."

"Oh, I don't care about that. But I think he's upset you're *not* handling him."

Silence grabs the line for a beat, two.

"It's only been a month," Elle goes on, softer this time. "You okay?"

"Emotionally, yes. Ian and I are over. But dating someone you work with—someone you can't stop working with even after you split—is like getting bangs. It seems like a great idea and then three months later, you're crying into a bucket."

Elle's delighted laughter makes me smile. "You've been living with me too long."

We hang up, and I settle into the drive, unsure of whether I want it to go faster or slower as we pass familiar buildings and streets.

I have a career in entertainment I've built myself. Playbills with my name on them, even if I was only onstage twenty minutes a night. An actual apartment in New York. Friends I can count on.

But life is about to ask me a question.

I feel it in the air.

And right now, the air has me tingling.

Too soon, the car pulls up the driveway, and I punch in the gate code. The winding drive is the same as I remember, but now there's a second laneway that runs parallel on the other side of the fence. It runs up the property and around the house.

Interesting.

On that loop, a valet is parking cars, and there are at least fifty—mostly expensive late-model, with a few classics thrown in.

"Go to the front," I instruct my driver.

By the time I'm out of the car, Haley's already emerging from the double doors. She's wearing a yellow dress that's feminine and no-nonsense at once and looks gorgeous with her dark hair. I can't help but grin.

But my gaze lands on her round stomach, and I suck in a breath. "You look ready to pop."

"And you look great." She beams and folds me in a hug.

It feels good to hug her. These past couple of years, we've gotten closer even though I've been away. Strange how you can feel close to someone you never see except on occasional video calls.

"Annie!"

I pull back to see a tiny human in the doorway in

a green dress, pigtails in her dark hair and fists on her waist.

"You came for my party," she states.

The air vanishes from my lungs. My half sister isn't a toddler anymore. She's got Haley's bow mouth and amber eyes like mine and the last time I saw Sophie in person, she couldn't say a complete sentence.

All of which makes it hard to respond in kind.

"Sure did. But I heard it was Dad's party."

She shakes her head vigorously. "It's for me. Those are my friends." She points back over her shoulder and I swallow the laugh.

Her eyes brighten as she inspects me. "What's in there?" She points to the weekender bag the limo driver set by the door.

"A party dress. You want to see?"

"Uh-huh."

Then she turns on her heel and takes off back into the house.

Haley rolls her eyes. "Well, that's Sophie. She broods like your dad and laughs like me but we still don't know where the energy comes from."

"I'm sure we'll have time to hang out later. Anyway, sorry I'm late. We sat on the tarmac two hours because of a baggage issue. Looks like the party's started," I say as I nod toward the cars.

"It has, but the path to your room is clear if you'd like to get changed."

Haley starts to grab my bag, but I step in. "Don't you dare."

She leads the way through the house. Sounds of the party drift through the hallways, but aside from glimpses of stylish figures wearing casual suits and chic summer dresses in the kitchen and living room and patio beyond, there's no one in our path as we head upstairs.

"We're so glad you came," Haley starts. "I know you've been busy working on your new show."

"It's not every day Dad launches a music label. I never thought he'd go through with it."

"Me either. He's talked about it long enough, but I figured it was his way of complaining about his former label when he sees Mace and the guys from the band."

When I push open the door of my old bedroom, I freeze.

It's exactly the way I remember.

My music boxes line the shelves, the same duvet covers the bed.

I set my bag down and swallow the emotion that rises up.

I had been expecting it to hit when I saw the house, but for some reason, it's coming now with my stepmom watching me, one hand on her swollen stomach and her lips softly curved.

"This will always be your home," she says firmly. "No matter what."

"Thank you," I say and mean it.

Haley leaves, and I turn back to my suitcase, pulling out the backless purple dress with a deep V neckline and the strappy sandals that show off my legs, toned from dancing.

Thanks to being on stage eight times a week, I have makeup and hair down to a science. Once my eyeliner is done, my lips are slicked a coral pink in honor of summer, and my hair waves down my back, I step into the dress.

This place may not have changed, but I have. Now that the run of my show is over, my hair's back to its natural dark red and starting to grow out, still a couple of inches past my shoulders. My body was always lean, but now it's strong from dance and long hours of rehearsing. I don't have ready access to a pool since the building Elle and I live in doesn't have one, but I do try to hit the gym three days a week and eat well in order to sustain the pace of my lifestyle.

Because if there's one thing I've learned about being in this industry?

You have to want it—more than anything.

Even then, your dreams find ways to mess with you.

When I head downstairs, there are a ton of people in the great room and spilling out to the patio. I scan the room, but most faces are only vaguely familiar at best. I don't see my dad or Haley or even Sophie.

At the bar, I accept the offered glass of champagne from the attractive bartender who checks me out with a grin as he passes me the glass, but I'm thrown when two strong arms band around me from behind.

I spin around and delight surges through me. "Uncle Ryan!"

I fold him in a hug.

"Good to see you, kid. How long are you staying?"

"Just for the weekend. I couldn't miss the party."

"I didn't know you were coming."

Surprise works through me, but before I can comment, there's a light clinking of glasses and we follow the crowd through the open doors to the patio.

My dad is standing in the center of the crowd, a polite circle formed around him.

My hand tightens on the stem of the champagne flute.

He's wearing a dark jacket over his jeans, his hair casually styled without any hint of gray. The hard cut of his jaw and nose haven't changed, but I swear there're more lines when his eyes crinkle against the sun.

I haven't been home since first semester at Vanier, though I talk to Haley on video or audio calls at least once a month. Sophie makes appearances almost every time, but my dad does drive-bys only on occasion—as if he, like me, knows things between us aren't okay.

I know he offered to meet me halfway after Tyler got hurt, but it felt as if he saw what happened to Tyler as proof I fucked up by moving to New York, by straying from his protection.

So I focused on achieving my dreams on my own. I've survived months I didn't know if I'd make enough money to keep the lights on, weeks of ice baths after endless dance rehearsals until my limbs ached. All for the chance to be on stage.

Even though I'm not yet sure what I want to say to him, he must have some idea what he wants to say to me since he invited me here.

That he was wrong would be a good start.

"Thank you for coming," he says to the crowd. "The music industry is changing in ways it never has. The old labels have consolidated, adapted, but they're not meant for this new world. They put money in the pockets of executives. This new label is going to change all of it. Put the music and the musicians back in the..." His gaze meets mine, and his words trail off as an expression of disbelief takes over his face.

I suck in a slow breath as I connect the pieces.

Haley's emphatic words.

Ryan's surprise.

My dad didn't invite me. He didn't even know I was coming.

He clears his throat and continues. "Back in the middle, where they belong. Enjoy yourselves today and celebrate with us. Not only for the label, but for music."

Applause and cheers rise up, but I barely hear them.

The patio is suddenly too loud, too stimulating.

I need to get out of here.

I turn away, taking a long, urgent drink of champagne as my gaze lands on the pool house.

Except it's not a pool house anymore.

There's a decorative iron gate—open, for now—between the patio and the structure, and the building itself has been renovated, expanded to twice its original size.

I head toward the building, winding through the crowd, and a parking lot on the other side comes into view through the hedge of shrubs angled to afford privacy and separate the two areas. The main entrance to the building is off the parking lot, meaning the door by the pool is a side entrance, likely intended for family only and accessible solely from this direction.

My dad would never want someone else's business in his backyard. But his business, with a literal door he can close, a way to access it anytime and close it just as easily...

That he'd like.

The door is etched glass, and I turn the handle, expecting it to be locked, but it gives.

For all the noise outside, it's quiet inside. I step inside to find sleek off-white carpet with geometric designs.

I follow the short hallway that opens into the old pool house bedroom, which is now a lobby unlike any I've ever seen. Display cases line the walls, but instead of rows of hard seats, there's a couch and comfy chairs, plus two more hot-desk workstations on the far side.

A more permanent-looking desk—probably for reception—is where the bed used to be.

Feelings slam into me, the scent of sun and cedar I must be making up from memory.

It takes a second for me to notice a curvy, dark-haired woman younger than me behind the desk. Her hair is in braids, her smile wide. "I know you. You're Annie Jamieson. I recognize you from photos," she says, her voice vibrating with excitement. "I'm Shay."

"Nice to meet you."

"You must've come to look around. Good idea to wait until after the rush." She gestures toward the desks. "These are for visiting artists and staff. On each side of the hall there's a studio, an office, and a meeting room. It's for music, not luxury. Function, not form. But I think it's beautiful." She says the last part under her breath, as if she's rebelling by merely voicing the words.

"You saw it before the renovations," Shay goes on. "Do you miss what it was?"

Feelings slam into me—nostalgia, longing, regret. "Sometimes. But things are meant to change."

I walk down the hall and try the handle of the first studio door. It's locked.

When I look across at the second studio, I see movement on the other side of the door. I try the handle, and it gives, opening soundlessly. Laughter fills my ears.

There's a man standing straight, a woman pressed close to him. I clear my throat.

They both turn toward me.

The woman's beautiful, but it's not her I'm looking at.

It's him.

Strong legs are encased in indigo jeans. Broad shoulders stretch the black jacket, which is rolled up at the sleeves to reveal swirls of inky tattoos. The top two buttons of the matching shirt are undone. And above that…

There's a face so familiar it hits me in the gut.

Not because it's impossible to scan an entertainment newsfeed without seeing him.

No, the gut punch is because I've kissed that face. Dreamed about it.

I've felt it between my thighs.

He was a man when he left on tour, but he's more than that now. I see it in every hard line of his body, every shadow on his face.

"You surprised us." The woman laughs, reminding me we're not alone. She keeps talking, but I don't get any of it.

Tyler's dark eyes intensify as he takes me in. His chin drops as he starts a slow survey at my heels, drags up my legs, lingering at the top as if he can see what's beneath my dress.

Or he's remembering it.

There shouldn't be so many feelings colliding in my chest.

"And you are?" the woman asks me, jerking me back.

I should've had something to eat on the plane. That feeling in the air, that sense of unease lifting the hairs on my neck…

He's standing in front of me wearing black and an unreadable expression.

Tyler Adams might've changed in two years, but so have I. I'm better at hiding my heart instead of wearing it on my sleeve.

But that doesn't stop me from draining my champagne before answering.

"Too old for this shit."

6

———

Tyler

There are different kinds of famous.

There's the famous that puts asses in seats at your latest show and fan pages in your results when you type your name into an internet search bar.

Then, there's the famous where you can't cross a street without being ambushed. Even industry insiders rush you, only they do it with air kisses and stories rather than with selfie requests.

After a year of touring and an EP, I'm still closer to the first camp. But the man hosting this party will always rule the second.

The patio's decked out with high-end décor and higher-end guests. The king of rock has come out of retirement to start a label, and everyone wants a front-row seat.

It's not Jax I'm looking for.

I search the crowd for Annie, and I finally spot her at the bar. It takes a few minutes for me to get to her, as I'm slowed by industry types who try to suck me into conversations.

"I didn't think I'd see you," I comment once I fight my way through.

At the sound of my voice, Annie turns.

I've played big stages, but the moment those golden eyes fringed in dark lashes find me, I'm a fucking newb.

At being a musician.

At being a man.

Her dark-purple dress hugs her figure, and I can't stop staring. Not because she looks fantastic, though she does, but because it's been so long since I've seen her in person.

"I didn't think I'd walk in on you in the pool house with a girl. Again." Her voice is low and smooth, with a hint of self-mocking. "Somehow, that wasn't the most awkward encounter I've had this afternoon."

Annie looks past me at the crowd.

I follow her gaze but don't see where it's landed. "In that case, I owe you a drink."

"It's an open bar."

"Fine, I'll buy you two."

That earns me a reluctant smile as Annie orders

a sparkling water and I get a ginger ale.

"I wasn't sure you'd be here, either," she admits as she takes the drink from the bartender. "Heard you were in the studio in LA."

"I'm on a break."

"For?" She sidesteps to let a man brush past her heading toward the bar.

I turn it over before answering. "Sanity."

The fabric of my dark jacket absorbs the sun, and I'm heated from that and her attention.

She lifts her glass. "To sanity, then."

"Amen."

We both drink.

I swore if I saw the first woman I ever loved again —*when* I saw her again—it would be like seeing an old friend.

But as my gaze runs over her pale skin and slick lips, it doesn't feel like that at all.

It feels like every scar I've ever had is new again.

"Ooof," comes a noise from knee height as something slams into my legs.

Sophie peers up with bright eyes from under dark bangs. Her little elbows try their best to clamp around my knees. "I got you, Uncle Tyler."

"And what will you do with me?"

Sophie's round face scrunches. "Cheese."

"You're going to turn me into cheese."

"No." Giggles rack her little body, vibrating

through my legs. "There's cheese up there." She points to a high top table a few feet from the bar, lowering her voice as if we're conspiring together.

Then she shrieks, delighted, as I boost her up on my hip.

"Does Annie like cheese?" Sophie asks as I walk us to the table.

"I have watched your sister inhale her body weight in cheese fries."

I let Sophie pick out a few chunks of cheese with a toothpick before setting her back down.

"Want anything?" When I start to pass Annie a plate, her fingers brush mine.

"Be careful. Tyler has an ouchie," Sophie intervenes from around a bite of Manchego.

Annie takes the plate but stares at the black rose on my hand, the vines winding down over my knuckles. "I heard it was three months before you started playing."

When she saw my hand last, it was a mess of still-red gashes. Now, it's covered in white lines, but the ink is all most people see.

"I was reduced to singing for eighty-six days. The guys I toured with mocked me endlessly. Got my first surgery when we came back to the States."

There was still pain, but at least I had more control of my fingers. I remember the hope that came from the surgery, thinking it would be a cure-all, only to realize it had made a modest difference at best.

"Did you tell the band to suck it?"

"Among other things." My lips twitch at the corner and hers curve to match.

Suddenly, I'm remembering the feel of them under mine. I'm thinking of the things that mouth has done to me. The things I never had a chance to do with it.

I wish I could say we made it work with me on tour and her in New York, or even that we tried.

But that would be a lie.

She didn't want me.

Not that she said as much. But overnight, our relationship was reduced to stilted texts, rushed phone calls squeezed into the margins of our lives.

The shows and the work and the relentless schedule were something I ended up grateful for because they kept me from thinking too much about what could've been.

I was going through some shit—trauma, plus shock, chased by some depression. Some days felt fine, like cracked pieces of broken ground after an earthquake settling together over time. Some days, it was hell.

"How hard was it to learn to pick with your other hand?" Her question brings me back.

To the rest of the world, I'd diminish it. The long

hours late at night, early in the morning, learning my craft from scratch until I was better than most, if not as good as I once was.

"Hard."

Her eyes color with compassion over the rim of her glass.

I'm not the same person I was two years ago. Most people would agree that I'm more, given my career, my recognition, the gold album I recorded with the help of half a dozen nimble-fingered studio musicians.

But in some ways, I'm less.

We've both moved on, and I don't blame her for our breakup. I was impossible to be around.

Still. I wish she hadn't been so quick to ask me to leave, and so willing to accept when our schedules made it harder to connect.

Because she didn't want us as much as I did.

So maybe I do blame her.

My gaze drops to a chain glinting dully in the sunlight and disappearing beneath the already-low V of her dress.

When she shifts, I catch a glimpse of the end of it. Instead of a ring and a rose, there's pearl-encrusted pendant.

Because it's not my chain.

And she's not my girl.

There are plenty of women who'd beg for a

chance to satisfy me, including the one I met at this party who was exploring the studio with me when Annie walked in.

I clear my throat. "I heard you're writing a new show." I haven't been keeping tabs on her, but I get the big developments from my roommate in LA, since she and Beck are still friends.

"We're pitching funders later this summer, but there've been some problems." A frown crosses her face. "I wasn't sure I should come to the party at all because of my deadline. Now it turns out Haley invited me and my dad didn't know I'd be here."

I blink. "You're joking."

She shakes her head, her hair slipping over one shoulder as she scrunches her face in embarrassment. "No. I guess two years is a long time to be gone."

The pieces click into place.

That was her other surprise today.

Jax hasn't mentioned her to me since he and I reconnected after my tour, but I figured it was for my benefit, not because he hadn't seen her either.

Someone calls Annie's name and she looks past me.

"Looks like Uncle Ryan wants to catch up. I should go."

"It was good to see you, Six," I say and mean it.

I don't know why I slide in the nickname. Habit.

Not to see if there's a flicker behind her eyes.

"You too, Tyler."

But as she brushes past me, I can't help thinking Annie's the one on the outside looking in.

And it feels wrong.

"Congrats," I tell Jax after Haley takes Sophie for some quiet time. The party has started to die down, and only Jax's closer contacts and friends remain.

I lift the glass of bourbon he pushed on me to toast him at the bar inside the house. "You have everything you could want. A beautiful family. A bourbon brand. And now a label, the great 'fuck you' to the studio that fucked you first."

The man of the hour has stripped out of his jacket and is now wearing a black T-shirt and black pants and cowboy boots. When I first arrived, I offered to get him a hat, and he smirked while Haley laughed and murmured something that sounded like "midlife crisis."

"You've been in this business long enough to know this life doesn't come without sacrifices." He shakes his head. "Speaking of, how's recording going with Zeke?"

I frown. "I'm halfway through an album, but I've been slowing down."

The past few months in studio, I've gotten down four finished tracks. But they don't make me happy the way music used to make me happy.

"Come record with me."

I swirl my drink. "I'm on a five-year contract for three albums with a studio option."

"Which means your ass belongs to Zeke."

"My ass belongs to no one."

I've paid off my dad's medical bills, and I'm planning to buy a place by the ocean where it's warm. Zeke's sending me new songs I have zero interest in recording. Plus prods about self-promotion. Like even on break, I can placate the record execs by dropping a few poolside selfies. Hashtag tortured artist or whatever the PR team emails.

I rub my left hand over my neck, mostly to feel the mess of tingling and soreness that sets in from flexing my fingers.

Jax's gaze narrows. "It hurts."

"Scar tissue's a bitch. It doesn't like the cold or vibration or days that end in Y."

I could write for days about the moods of a damned appendage, one that intermittently has numbness and searing pain, that makes me regret I ever took for granted a second of what I used to do.

What I'll do again soon.

"I head out the doors to the patio, the easy laughter of the stragglers standing in familiar groups drawing me toward them. When my gaze lands on the former pool house beyond, I stop.

My mentor pulls up at my side.

"You should've started this label years ago," I say.

Jax only shrugs. "Things happen at the right time. May not be your right time or mine, but they happen when they're meant to."

I crane my neck towards the gardens edging the patio. "There a Buddhist statue around here I haven't seen?"

Jax laughs, his deep voice rumbling. "Problem with the label is I've got some guys booking the space, but we need new sounds. New voices."

"You haven't found anyone." I'm surprised to hear that because I know dudes who'd fly from LA in a heartbeat to record at Jax's studio.

"I have one kid, but he's got an attitude, and with all the legal and financial red tape, I haven't had time to work with him. Sophie's been acting out lately, and Hales is due in six weeks."

"Supervising a teenager can't be that hard. I practically taught myself."

He eyes me up. "If it's that simple, you try getting him to lay down something good."

I'm only half listening, my gaze finding Annie across the patio. She's standing in a group that includes Mace, Jax's former bassist Brick, and Brick's fiancée, Nina.

"Haley invited her." Awe and weariness twine in Jax's multimillion-dollar voice.

"How long is she staying?"

"No clue. Haven't got my wife pinned down long enough to ask her which direction the sun's rising and setting in, either."

I take a sip of the bourbon. It's actually not bad. "You and Annie should've made up sooner."

"I've tried."

"Try harder."

"Kids aren't that easy, Tyler. Someday, you'll see."

I always figured the rift between them came from Annie's "try anything twice" attitude and Jax's fierce protectiveness, along with a dose of stubbornness on both sides. Regardless, I hate that Jax and I made up when he and his own daughter haven't.

I could fix it.

The thought takes hold and won't let go.

I turn to face my former mentor. "Give me two weeks. I'll get a decent track out of your aspiring artist in the studio."

Jax chuckles. "I assume you want something in return."

I drain the rest of my bourbon and set the glass on the nearby table the caterers have started cleaning.

"You take care of your problems with your real kid. Tell Annie you're sorry," I go on under the weight of Jax's stare. "That you're an idiot and you fucked up two years ago and fans can't buy you a scrap of perspective when it comes to the people in your life."

When his amber eyes spark, and it's unsettling how much they're like Annie's. "You're serious. Why do you care enough to give me two weeks of your time?"

"Because I made things harder for her."

"That's the only reason."

"That's the only reason," I echo.

But as he turns to go back inside, I yank off my jacket, feeling overheated once again.

7

Annie

I'm ripped from my dreams in my former bedroom the next morning. For once, it's not because I've got an idea for a song or a line I need to write down.

It's because of shrieking in the distance.

I tug on tailored black shorts and a white tank top I brought from New York and head downstairs, but by the time I get there, it's quiet. The morning sun spills in through the huge kitchen windows and the slider doors. The only sign of life is Haley moving around the cavernous space, making coffee in a flowing black top.

"Everyone alive?" I ask.

She turns, smiling. "Your dad took Sophie to daycare. She's always loved it, but recently, she's not a fan. Oliver doesn't like her and she doesn't like Teddy."

She's moving slowly toward the fridge, either from tiredness or her gigantic belly, and I spring into action. "You sit down. I'll make breakfast."

I grab a carton of eggs, some bacon, and cheese for good measure, plus a huge frying pan from a cupboard, before turning on the gas.

"Why did you invite me without telling Dad?" I ask over my shoulder. "I shouldn't be mad at a pregnant woman. But I am."

"It was kind of a dick move, but my heart was in the right place. I wasn't sure I could get you both here with your guards down otherwise."

I drop four strips of bacon into the pan. "I shouldn't have lied to him—to both of you—about school, but he overreacted when he found out."

"I get why you feel that way. I do. But if you look for evidence to be angry with someone, you'll always find it. What kind of place would the world be if we stopped weighing and measuring mistakes, and using those measurements to define our relationships? Maybe we'd be able to choose how we want to feel about other people from love instead of judgement."

I crack eggs into the remaining half of the simmering pan, watching the whites spread.

"How come Dad has eight years on you, but you're the sensible one?"

She snorts. "The question for you," she continues, "isn't whether you want to be part of this family, but how you want to be part of it. I'm the one with the least say, but for what it's worth, I'd love for you to be here to celebrate days like yesterday. To feel like this is your home when you need one. I want to see you and your dad laugh when Sophie names her trucks after eighties bands and races them down the hallway. I want all of us to raise a glass to you when you conquer the world, or when you go down trying."

I don't know how I'm going to settle things with my dad, but hearing how Haley talks, seeing the three of them together, knowing I'll have a new half brother or sister soon, I want to be a part of it.

The plates are in the same cabinet they used to be, and I retrieve two.

I finish cooking our breakfast and set both plates in front of us. Haley chuckles as she takes in the flower design I made on her plate with syrup.

"I figured no one's done this for you lately."

She smiles. "You'd be right. Does this mean you're not mad anymore?"

"Jury's still out."

I drop into the seat across from her, and we dig in.

"How's the musical coming? You told me you're working with mostly the same team, but you and your writing partner are leading this time instead of following." She reaches for her mug.

Nervous energy has me swallowing an extra big bite of egg. "It's going to be amazing. Creatively, it's been going well until now. We have ten songs written, but I'm struggling to drag it across the finish line. It's not like I can't write anything. But nothing seems to matter enough. Nothing feels good enough or big enough or *true* enough."

I've spent hours a day trying to get myself out of this rut—reading, going for walks, brainstorming... I even bought a dream journal which, so far, succeeded in telling me I spend way too much of my subconscious thinking about pastries.

"The end is always the hardest."

"Right? And I've been distracted because the funders..." I savagely bite into a piece of bacon. "The money is complicated. We have a reading scheduled with prospective funders at the end of the summer. Miranda and I thought it would be a slam dunk, but it's looking harder every day."

Because Ian was supposed to fund this.

Ian was not, however, supposed to fuck another woman, particularly the afternoon I walked into his apartment unannounced.

My stepmom takes a long sip of decaf, staring

thoughtfully at her empty plate. "You need a change of scenery."

I lift my brows in surprise. "Here?"

"It's a huge house. There's plenty of room without stepping on anyone's toes. Plus, you always loved the patio in the summer."

Dad and I might kill each other.

But my gaze drops to the hand she rubs over her stomach. "This guy or girl has been keeping me up. They're not due for another six weeks, but I don't think we're going to last that long. Sophie's started waking in the middle of the night, and your dad's been busy with unexpected administration issues for the label."

Compassion washes over me.

"Let me help," I hear myself say. "I can't stay for six weeks, but maybe two? I can flex my work around watching Sophie and whatever you need."

Her face relaxes. "I'd love that. And your dad would, too."

"Let's not go crazy," I say dryly, and she laughs again.

I take our plates to the dishwasher and look out the kitchen windows over the patio. There are a couple of cars I can make out through the hedges separating us from the small tree-lined parking lot. "Who's at the label this early?"

"Probably Shay. Maybe someone's booked in to record."

"Okay. I'll catch up with you later."

I head outside and go to the label, letting myself through the side door and into the lobby.

The girl behind the desk is the same one from yesterday. She's facing away, humming a catchy song. She turns around and spots me, startled, and pulls off her headphones. "Annie! Can I help with something? I'm supposed to make sure everyone signs in. I know it's weird to ask you to, but... I got a new book and everything," she says proudly.

I write on the fresh sheet of paper. "Sure. No one else has signed in yet?"

"Studio One is booked all week starting at noon. Your dad is holding studio two for his own artists. Today you're our first guest."

I head down the hall, bracing myself as I glance into Studio Two.

I know I won't see the same thing I saw yesterday—that woman and Tyler—but my stomach tightens anyway.

The studio is empty.

I continue to the offices. The door of the one with Dad's name on it is closed, but the second's is open.

It's sparse but stylish. There's a desk, a potted palm in one corner, and a beautiful piano.

Unable to resist, I cross to the piano, skimming a

finger over the ivory keys and playing a few bars of the song I've been working on all month.

"Don't stop now, it was just getting good."

I jump at the sound of Tyler's voice, spinning to see him emerge from under the desk wearing jeans, a long-sleeved shirt, and a crooked grin.

"What are you doing here?" I ask.

"Trying to plug in. I need to hardwire the internet for a virtual meeting later. I'm babysitting your dad's new shining star, who is coming by"—from under the edge, I see him check his watch—"twenty minutes ago, supposedly."

Some musicians make their fans feel welcome, invite them into their lives and homes on social media.

Tyler's always held them at a distance.

The paparazzi love him. The cleverer he gets at evading, the more they stalk. I empathize with both sides—him wanting privacy and fans dying to know more about this man who lights up a stage with his earnest talent.

They want to know who Tyler Adams is.

Can't say I blame them.

Seeing him at the party affected me. Not in a jealousy kind of way, but because catching up with him after reminded me of the deliberate, thoughtful guy I grew up with. Except there was a new dimension to him, too. An ease, with himself and the world, that he didn't have when we were together.

Just because we've barely spoken in two years doesn't mean we can't be civilized adults now. There's no rule that say you need to hate your ex.

"Let me try." I brush past him and tug the phone from the pocket of my jean shorts and set it down.

It's a tight fit under the desk as I crouch, but there's a hole to thread the cord through, and I work away at it.

"Thanks. Didn't know this office came with tech support," Tyler says, his voice muffled from above the desk.

I flip him off and he chuckles.

My phone rings on the desk.

"Ian," he reads off the display, and I stiffen.

"Do not get that."

"You playing hooky from work?"

I stick my head out, glaring up at him. "Tyler, I'm serious."

"Not a work call. Boyfriend, then. Wonder if he knows you're ducking him."

The casual words drag me back to the past.

The first time we broke up, when he left me after high school, it was a rip. A violent tear.

The second time was a loosening, little by little. Day by day. My heart wasn't ripped from my chest; it was pried—with a blunt, persistent instrument—

worked under one edge at a time, until nothing remained to hold it in its place.

Unreturned phone messages thanks to demanding rehearsals. Half-hearted texts after long flights. Two months of slow descent, the beginning of the end.

But it was what I wanted when I told him to take that tour. For his life to go on, and mine too.

We've both moved on. I resist the urge to rub at my chest, the dull ache there as my fingers rush to finish what I started so I can get out of here, get relief from the way his presence affects me.

The cord finally clicks into place, and I grunt with triumph before I rock back on my heels to take him in.

"What about you?" I challenge, thinking of how I walked in on him yesterday. "Is that why you never post on social—so you can keep a bunch of women in different cities who want to think they're the only one? It's not original, but it's effective."

Tyler drops into the task chair. He props an elbow on the armrest, displaying the threads of ink that wind up his arm. I swear there are more than there were two years ago. I try to ignore the fact that his perfect denim-clad hips, those strong legs, are at eye level.

"I don't post pics with women because it's not my 'brand'." The self-mocking in his voice and the air quotes make me blink. "Marketing sent me a sheet with these adjectives about how the label thinks I should appear."

I stand, then sink my hips back against the desk. I realize too late I'm still practically in his lap. "Let me guess—you're mysterious but earnest. Intense. Maybe even repressed, except when you're on stage."

"How'd you get a copy?"

I can't help laughing, and Tyler grins too. The familiarity of it washes over me.

"I didn't. But I know you. I know how you are on stage and when you're alone in a room. I know why fans go crazy for you, and I know the things they'd go crazier for if they knew."

The laughter in his eyes fades at the intimacy of my words.

Okay, acting civilized is one thing. Don't let this get weird, I chastise.

"So when are you heading back to LA?" I ask, dragging a finger along the surface of the desk for somewhere to look that's not his handsome face, the lines of his strong arms, or the hand covered in scars and new ink.

"I promised to help your dad out with his new protégé for a couple of weeks while I'm on break."

My gaze snaps to his. "You're not staying at the house." The horror in my voice would be funny under other circumstances.

"I have a hotel."

Relief has me sagging against the desk. "I might be sticking around a couple of weeks, too."

Those chocolate eyes spark so fast I almost think I've imagined it.

I'm here to clear my head for work and help Haley.

Tyler could be a distraction.

You think?

I can handle being around him for a few days. I'll probably barely see him.

It's not like high school, where we were bumping into each other in the kitchen, by the pool, every day in class.

"This place is pretty epic," Tyler notes, looking around.

"Right? It's so new. Haley told me they stripped it down to almost nothing before rebuilding."

"Not nothing." Tyler nods toward the ceiling.

I crane my neck to look up, spotting the same thing he has. "The rafter."

One of the beams from the original pool house is still visible, painted to match the white ceiling and spanning this office and the next one.

"You can always start over, but you can never erase the past," I murmur.

"Do you want to?"

I look back at Tyler, one brow lifted under a fall of dark hair.

Those words have me thinking of us again. How we might have grown up and moved on with our lives, but we can't forget what we were.

"No," I say at last. "I don't."

Tyler tugs at a drawer, which glides open to reveal nothing except a container of paper clips. He pulls out a paper clip and unbends the end of it. "This Ian of yours. He meet your dad and Haley?"

I frown at the sudden change in subject. "No."

Tyler moves the chair toward me an inch, two, then hooks the end of the paper clip in the belt loop of my jeans. "A real man meets his girl's parents."

He's close enough his scent invades my senses. It's the sunshine and cedar I remember, with a smoky edge.

"Does a real man sneak out her window so her parents don't find out he spent the night?" I counter, thinking of prom, when he took Carly to the dance— when I slept in his arms after and made him promise not to leave.

Tyler's gaze narrows.

If I didn't know it was crazy, I'd think he was worked up about Ian.

I don't need to tell him we're broken up, because that'll only invite more questions when it's none of his business and I really don't want to talk about it with Tyler.

He rises from his chair, leaning in to murmur at my ear. "The next time I visit your room at night, I promise I'll use the door after."

He walks out, leaving the paperclip dangling from my shorts.

8

Tyler

"**Y**our pinch harmonics are sloppy," I state. From his seat on the stool across the studio, the kid Jax recruited stares at me with dead eyes. "Can't you fix it with the board?"

"I could. But you're playing it wrong. Play it right, no one's gotta fix it."

It's my first day of babysitting, and the analogy's not far off. I figured I'd help the kid get the guitar and vocals for a track, but everything's either wrong or a pain in the ass.

When he gets up from his stool, I demand, "Where are you going?"

He holds up his hands. "Need a smoke break."

Was this what I was like working with Jax?

No. No way.

Could be I'm pissier than usual. Probably

because my hand's been hurting more in the months since I left the tour—or maybe I have more time to think about it—and Zeke called and left a belligerent voicemail to say he hadn't heard back from me about the songs.

I followed up with an email telling him I'd thought he sent them as a joke and I was still laughing.

Fifteen minutes later, there was an email from marketing noting I hadn't posted anything on social since a picture Beck took in LA and I'm overdue.

I go out to the front room to ask Shay about the schedule, and she pulls her headphones off her ears.

"What're you listening to?" I ask.

"Local artists. There's a lot of talent here. One of my favorites is actually playing tonight at Valor. And," she goes on, both brows rising up her face, "they have two for one drinks. I can text you the details."

"Thanks." I'm not planning on going to a local gig and the appeal of two for one drinks has long stopped being a motivator, but I can't shoot down her enthusiasm.

She punches my number into her phone, but I'm already looking up as the kid comes back in the front door, smelling like smoke and brushing past me to the studio.

I follow him in. "Let's try the track again. And clean it up this time."

"You wanna show me what you had in mind with your fucked-up hand?" the kid drawls.

I narrow my gaze. "Give me the guitar."

He does, and I hook it around my neck.

I'm going to regret this for the next two days, but I don't even care.

I play the passage like I'm on stage at MSG with no one to cover my ass—including the pinch harmonics.

My hand is on fire, and not in a good way. It hurts like hell. If I had to play an entire set like this, the muscles would give out and I'd have cramps for days.

Thank God I don't. Only enough to shut this dumb kid up.

It won't always be like this, I remind myself.

When I'm done, he's silent.

I shove the guitar in his face. "I can play it with my fucked-up hand, so you can play it with your fucked-up attitude. Again."

By the time we have something passable, it's after dark, and I'm beyond ready to get away from this asshole.

For a moment, I debate calling one of the guys I toured with or the friends I met on the road. They'd remind me what it's like to be around people who take their careers seriously.

On the way to my car, I almost run over the kid, who's leaning into the hedge that runs along the iron fence separating the pool.

My gaze fixes on Jax's patio, and I take in what he's staring at—a woman swimming.

Naked.

The visual hits me like a knockout punch—not because it's any woman, but because it's one in particular.

"Keep walking." I bite out the words, and he jumps, eyes widening as if he's listening for the first time today.

"Chill, man. She's swimming naked. Clearly she wants someone to look."

"Let me guess. You don't have a girlfriend."

He shrugs. "Like to keep my options open."

He heads for his car, where I should be going too, but I reverse directions and go back into the studio, using my swipe key to go out the side door.

Because I should tell her she might be spotted. Not for any other reason.

I let myself in the gate and cross to the cabana. I grab a towel.

When Annie rises up out of the water, shoving her long hair out of her wet face in a way that makes my throat dry, I'm there. "Run out of clean suits already?"

Annie takes me in, hands gripping the edge of

the pool as her eyes widen in surprise. "It's late. Needed to clear my head, and I didn't think anyone would notice."

"Just my shit-for-brains kid in the studio. You made his day."

She smiles, a flash of white in the dark.

Earlier when she told me she was sticking around, I was glad and frustrated at once.

Because even though there's nothing between us, sharing the same space with her felt right. As if part of me that'd been missing suddenly clicked back into place.

No matter what Jax said, I can coexist with the woman who ripped my heart out.

I can even do it without staring at her ass as she bends under the desk. Or peering over the edge of the pool to see how much of her body is lit by the soft blue lights.

"You coming out?" I ask lightly.

"You turning around?"

"Nothing I haven't seen."

"Maybe it's changed."

Those three words have me dying to know if she's right, if she's different since the last time I touched her, held her, made her pant my name.

I shut my eyes and hold out the towel.

I hear the sound of water dripping as she shifts out, then her voice, inches away. "Thanks."

She steps closer, and I wrap her in the towel. "You're not wrong, though. I only packed for a weekend. I'm going to have to raid my old closet, assuming anything in there still fits."

Her breasts are nearly pressed against my chest through the towel, and I imagine using the terry fabric to drag her body against mine.

"I'll give you ten bucks to wear your Oakwood uniform for a day."

She laughs. "Make it twenty and I'll think about it."

I open my eyes to find her studying me. Water drips over her shoulders, and there's a drop on the middle of her lower lip I want to brush off.

It's hard to remember why I can't, especially with the visual of her in a pleated skirt and tight shirt firmly in my head.

"So, how's it going in the studio with my dad's protégé?" she prompts, and I force myself to focus as she takes the towel from me and knots it around her breasts.

"Brutal. Kid's a pain in the ass. So why'd you need to clear your head? Your dad? Or the boyfriend?" I ask.

The boyfriend was not part of the updates Beck gave me, something he's going to eat shit for the next time we talk.

Though now I'm wondering why he didn't tell

me. If he thought I'd be jealous, I'm not. Not even close.

I'm over us, but that doesn't mean I want her with some guy who doesn't deserve her. And if she's avoiding him, it means something's wrong.

I will always want the best for her, because I loved her once. For a time that feels boundless, until I remind myself it's over.

Annie pulls her hair over one shoulder and wrings it out, sending drops of water splattering on the patio.

"Both," she answers at last.

It sounds like what she really needs is to get out of her head. I know that look, not because it's classic Annie, but because it's classic *me*.

I can be around her without rehashing the reasons we broke up, without obsessing over the messy perfection of the times we were together.

I'll prove it.

"Shay told me about a local concert. Go with me."

"Like a date?" Her brows shoot up.

"No, music police," I chastise. "Like I'm going out of my mind and something tells me you are too."

It's not an invitation—it's a challenge. She lifts her chin, like she knows it too. "Fine."

Annie meets me in my black Lexus nine minutes later.

As she shifts inside, I run my gaze over her black

skinny jeans, little heels, black tank. Her hair's still wet and piled on her head, but it looks intentional, especially with the addition of the dark rims around her eyes and red lips.

Play nice.

I force my attention to the driveway.

It's a quiet drive to the music hall, and we talk about easy subjects like who was at Jax's party, the crazy new sponsors Beck got for his Hollywood Life vlog, and whether Haley's new baby will be a boy or a girl.

"It's a boy," I tell her. "I have guy intuition."

"Definitely a girl," Annie decides. "Then Dad will have three and his head will literally explode."

I grin.

So far, so good.

I pull up halfway across the parking lot as I see the line of music fans waiting to be admitted. "I'm going to get mauled."

"You're not that famous," she scoffs.

"I'm pretty famous." I say it mostly to watch her roll her eyes.

I grab a jacket out of my car and drag it on over my T-shirt and jeans.

She inspects me and frowns. "The hair..."

"What's wrong with my hair?"

Annie dives into her little bag and comes back with something that looks like gel. She slicks back my hair. "There. No one would ever recognize you without this mess all over your face."

"Tell me how you really feel."

She laughs as we head for the doors. In the heels, she's tall, almost as tall as me. She nods to security, and it takes me a second to realize she's actually protecting me, standing between the line of people and me.

It's oddly sweet.

There are people whose job it is to keep me safe when I'm on the road. But when Annie does it, it feels different.

Once we get in, we head to the bar.

"The real reason I brought you is the two for one drinks."

"I see. Are you drinking tonight?"

"No. More for you."

She laughs and we both end up ordering water.

It feels good to get out. Having Annie next to me doesn't suck either.

No one knows me here, or her for that matter. It's freeing in a way I haven't felt free in months.

The headline act starts to play, and I focus on their up-tempo opening number instead of the woman at my side.

"They're not bad," I say to her when they pause between songs.

"They're better than not bad. Look how much they want to be up there. It's pouring off them."

I study the band, their energy. "Maybe these kids need a deal. I could fire Jax's dumbass kid and take them instead."

"Miranda Talbot, my writing partner, always says to find someone with a voice. That the rest you can develop."

"It's not enough to want it. You have to put in the work."

"Whatever your recipe, it's effective. I've seen your show."

I straighten in an instant. "Where?"

"London. Paris." Her mouth purses. "Seattle."

I'm speechless.

"I had to know you were okay," she goes on as if explaining herself.

It doesn't explain shit.

"Tell me why the woman who wanted me out of her life followed me around the world."

Her groan has the hairs on my neck standing up. "I didn't want you gone, Tyler. I wanted..."

"What?"

"I wanted you *back*. I wanted you to feel like yourself again."

I take a drink of water, wishing it was something with a kick.

"Sometimes, I wonder what would've happened

if you'd come on tour," I tell her. "Or if I'd stayed in New York. If we'd still be together now."

Annie shoots me a look. "It would've been a different end, that's all. You held me at a distance. You were the one who was hurt, but I was the one who felt helpless."

When I imagined her with me, I never considered that I wouldn't let her be with me the way she wanted to, the way she needed to.

The reckoning I had to have with myself was steep. The work and music and touring gradually broke me down, healed me.

I couldn't have done that with her there. I would've taken it out on her, used her, abused her.

We would've split anyway—if she hadn't stayed in New York, if I hadn't left.

Something loosens in my chest. I glance over at her, her face lit up in the lights as she watches the band, breathless and engrossed.

I lean in at the next break. "Tell me about your show."

Annie's face transforms. Any angst disappears, replaced by anticipation and genuine delight. "It's a fantasy story about a girl born without a heart, but she doesn't want anyone to know. So, she goes on a quest to get one—not because she wants to feel, but because she's worried her body will give out without it. And on the way, she meets all these people, including this guy who makes her realize she wants to feel after all."

I'm sucked in already. She's always had the power to fascinate me, to take my world and wrap it around her, like that towel by the pool, so she's at its center.

"And you'll star in it."

She shivers, her eyes sparkling in the dark. "I want that more than anything."

I want to press her, but she's scanning the room.

A number of people have their phones out, but the cameras aren't pointed at me.

"This show will make for some great clips," she says absently.

"They're at a concert and they're not even watching."

"They're involving people in their experience. It takes two seconds. No wonder you drive your marketing people crazy. Give me your phone."

I unlock it and hold it out.

"Now put an arm around me and look at the stage."

"You Annie Leibovitz all of a sudden?"

But I do as she asks, pulling her against me.

Instantly my body's on alert. She's slow curves and I want to drag the hem of that shirt up and trail my fingers along her skin. Turn my face into her neck and lose myself in her rose scent.

"Broody enough for your brand?" she teases, holding the screen out.

The image is a kick in the gut.

In it, Annie's looking at the camera, though in the darkness, it's hard to recognize her.

I'm watching the music like I'm distracted—by it or the girl in my arms, it's impossible to tell—but it's tense and natural at once, as if she's part of me, an extension of me.

I want to back that photo up, to save it. To preserve it somehow so I never lose it, or her.

"Marketing's gonna come in their pants," I say at last.

As I tuck the phone away—I'll post the pic when I get back to the hotel, because otherwise, we'll get swarmed—more than a few pairs of eyes are on us.

It's understandable. We might not be dating, but she's still fucking awesome. She's got the same wonder at the world, plus a confidence that's new. It's fascinating, and sexy.

"It's late," she says when the show wraps up and the patrons stream toward the doors. "I shouldn't have stayed out so long. Sophie's already not sleeping. I don't want to wake her up."

A warning flashes through my brain, one I promptly ignore thanks to the concert or her closeness or the fact that it feels as if we're the only people in the world despite the rest of the giddy crowd dispersing to the parking lot.

"My hotel's close. You can crash. I have to be at the studio early tomorrow anyway."

She doesn't answer, and when I clue into why, my abs tightening as the shitty reality comes back to me.

Not only is she not mine, she belongs to someone else.

"If it's the boyfriend you're worried about, I promise I won't touch you."

"Ian and I broke up."

If she didn't have my attention before, she does now. "What?" I glance back toward the building. "That time you went to the bathroom an hour ago?"

She waves a hand. "We ended it last month."

"And you didn't tell me about it yesterday because..."

Annie shakes her head. "Because it didn't matter."

I don't believe her.

It's not my business, but it feels as if it is. The concern I felt for her, the irritation and contempt towards this faceless guy is still there, but it's competing with something I've been ignoring.

The pull I've always felt when she's around.

Knowing she was with someone made it easier not to stare at her too long, to think about what used to be.

"Do you still have your bike?" she asks as she shifts inside the rental car.

"Yeah. It's in LA."

Annie shakes her head as she reaches for the seatbelt. "I always imagined you taking me on it."

Adrenaline surges through me.

"I imagined taking you on it too."

The way my voice drops leaves no question as to what I'm imagining.

Her hands freeze on the seatbelt, those full lips parting.

I force my attention out the windshield before she can reply, but as I pull out of the parking lot, it's all I can think about.

Her on my bike.

In my lap.

Bending her over my arm while I rock my hips into her, against her, that red hair trailing over the handlebars.

Because the moment she told me she was single, the rules changed.

Not the rules for what happens next between us, but the rules for what goes on in my twisted head.

We go back to my place, and she heads for the pullout couch in my suite.

But I stop her, tugging her toward the bedroom. "You're not sleeping on the couch."

I go to the dresser and grab a clean T-shirt,

tossing it at her. She lifts her hands in surprise, catching it. "Thanks."

"Sure."

I reach for the bottom of my shirt and strip it over my head, tossing it on the nearby armchair.

Her eyes widen on my body.

The last times we were together physically, I took my pain out on her. My fear. My frustration.

I want a chance to prove I'm not that guy anymore. Not because we have a future together, but because I want to show her the man I became while she wasn't looking.

I want to know if I can still make her scream.

"What's that?" Annie's attention drags to something across the room.

I turn and see the object leaning against the wall by the dresser, the one that's so familiar I barely notice it anymore.

"My guitar."

"You still have it."

"Of course I do. Twenty-four frets. Rosewood. I fucking love that guitar. Some love lasts a lifetime."

"Just not ours." She blinks fast. "I'll change in the bathroom."

She heads that way, closing the door quietly behind her, and I rub my good hand over my neck and wonder what the fuck I was thinking bringing her here.

I shift into bed in my boxer briefs and exhale the breath I've been holding for longer than I can count.

The way Annie looked at me a second ago, it was almost as if she was accusing me. Like the way I loved the guitar she gave me outlasted how I loved her.

It's not true. The words feel as if they're coming from inside me and outside at once.

But it is. I'm over her. I told myself that for the last two years, since before I believed it.

Eventually, I started to.

She returns a moment later, crawling in next to me. Her light floral scent has me itching to reach my good arm around her and tug her body against mine.

Instead, I fist my hand at my side.

I remember every time we've shared a bed.

From the first time after her party in high school when I wanted to know she was okay to the time after prom.

The time in her dorm room at Vanier when I made her come for the first time.

The hotel in LA when I showed up at her door, swore she meant everything, and we made love for hours.

I think about the beds I lay in alone, nameless hotels in cities I barely remember.

Getting to perform for big crowds, having money and fans and influence for the first time—at least a backup band that listened to me for once instead of the other way around—mattered, but not nearly as much as it should have.

In months of touring, the only woman who ever got me off was Annie Jamieson. Her face, her voice, her damned memory was the only one I wanted in my bed.

I never told anyone, and I'm sure as hell not going to tell her as we lie next to each other, staring at the ceiling, still buzzed from the music.

But her closeness has my heart thudding hard enough to bruise my ribs.

"I was thinking about what you said. How we wouldn't have lasted on the road, and it wouldn't have worked if I'd stayed." My words echo in the dark. "You found yourself in New York and I lost myself there."

For a moment, I wonder if Annie's already asleep, until I feel the bed sink as she turns toward me.

"I replayed it in my head a thousand times. What I could've done differently. Giving you more space, or less. Trying to make it work from a distance."

I exhale hard. "No. I wish I'd been better in those moments. The last few times we were together... it wasn't good. I hate that you'll always remember me like that."

I feel her inch closer, her breath lightly fanning my lips. "I remember we used to dream about this.

You having a recording career and me being on stage. And now we are. So it all worked out, right?"

The question in her voice has my chest tightening in a way that's dangerous.

"Yeah. It all worked out."

9

Annie

"**I** don't want to wear that." Sophie gives me pre-schooler side-eye, then runs across the room toward her toys.

I sit back on my heels, the dress clutched in my hands, and wish for caffeine.

I offered to take my half sister to daycare today before starting on my work, but it's proving harder than expected.

I scan her room, looking at the white furniture, the rainbow bedspread, the corner box of toys and puzzles where she's currently pulling things out, one after another.

"Hey, let's play a game," I decide. "If you can pick out all your school things, I'll sing you a song in the car."

Miracle of miracles, it works.

After dropping her off, I head to the café that used to be my favorite in high school and open my tablet.

When I emailed Miranda to say I'd be in Dallas a couple of weeks working, she agreed. I promised we'd email every day or two to talk progress.

There's another person I need to update, and I'm less optimistic about the response I'll get.

Most of the musical is scored, but some of the lyrics aren't finished. In particular, there's a song between the two main characters I can't get right.

Back in school, it always seemed that emotions flowed through me, desperate to get out. All I had to do was put them on a page.

But writing a musical isn't only about feeling—it's about story—a narrative that was born to be told through song, one that can only be fulfilled in that format.

Even though I was involved in this show from the earliest days—the idea was Miranda's and mine, and it started being crafted back the first semester we worked together on the other show—it's not something you can half-ass like an assignment for course credit and cross your fingers for a good grade.

Getting a new musical to the stage requires millions of dollars, and while there's not one way to get it right, there are so many ways to get it wrong.

Which is why I need to call Ian.

He didn't leave a message when he called yester-day, which is Ian-speak for "I'm too important to leave a message." But I can't put this off.

I hit his contact on my cell, my stomach clench-ing. The line rings, and I turn the coffee cup in my hand.

Voicemail kicks in and I take a breath before starting.

"Ian, it's Annie. Elle said you were looking for me. I wanted to let you know I'm staying in Dallas for a couple of weeks while I finish the book for the musical. Once Miranda and I are satisfied with it, we'll send it to you and the three of us can discuss it in advance of the reading. Despite...what happened between us, I assume you're still interested in being a primary funder, which is why I want to keep you as informed as possible. If you have any questions or concerns, you know where to reach me."

I click off, satisfied I got my point across.

It's a moment before I realize someone's stopped near my elbow. I glance up and nearly knock my tablet off the table.

"Pen!" I squeal as my friend breaks into a grin. I jump up and hug her familiar form, dressed in a cute black jumpsuit and wedge sandals. "What are you doing here? I thought you were traveling to cover entertainment news at the newspaper!"

"It's my parents' twenty-fifth wedding anniversary, and a bunch of our family's in town. So, I'm home for the week." My friend cuts a look toward the menu, and I scan the pastry cabinet while she orders. "What are you doing here?"

I tell her about my dad's party, that I decided to stay. "But my dad and I haven't really talked," I finish.

"Which is why you're here at the café, avoiding him and wearing clothes you bought junior year?"

"Not avoiding. Working." I glance down at my white tank top tucked into denim shorts. "And I didn't really pack for an extended stay, so I raided my high school clothes. They're tighter than I remember."

"Yes. And also, you look amazing."

I laugh.

Pen gets her drink, and I order a croissant.

"So, you using your dad's new studio while you're home?" she says once we're sitting back at the table.

"No, but Tyler's working with my dad."

She nearly spits out her coffee, laughing. "Tyler Adams, international music sensation, Prince of Oakwood, King of Vanier, Duke of Annie Jamieson's heart, is in Dallas."

She has the decency to lower her voice when she says it.

I break off a piece of the croissant and shift in my seat. "We went to a concert last night."

When he showed up at the pool, all frustrated

and gorgeous and making me remember how things used to be, I wanted to go with him even though it was a bad idea.

Plus, we had fun. God, we had so much fun, more than I've had in a long time.

His intensity's still there, but he has this new relaxedness too. He was always sure of how to act in the world because he figures out everything and everyone, but now it's like the wheels in his head aren't turning quite so fast, as though he's not so busy judging everything and everyone.

"I'm glad you guys are making nice. I remember how hard it was on you when he left." Pen's voice pulls me back. "Would you ever get back together?"

"No." The word comes out fast. "I'm not going near men for a long time."

Even if Tyler's more gorgeous than ever, and everything about him beckons me closer.

Lying in bed next to him last night, hearing his steady breathing, feeling his closeness, was not something I'd planned. But we'd had such a good time and I didn't want to wake up half the house by getting home late.

Saying yes to the innocent offer to crash left me with more than I bargained for.

"I know you and Ian dated for six months," Pen goes on.

"Meaning?" I arch a brow and she lifts both palms.

"Hot rebound sex. Hear me out," she goes on at my expression. "Tyler's fire. Always was, and he's only gotten hotter with age and the whole famous thing."

"He's not *that* famous."

She cringes. "If you're in Rolling Stone, you're famous. If you're playing a benefit concert this weekend in LA with four other Grammy-winning acts? You're famous. The point is, you're both unattached. You're in Dallas, and he's living in the pool house."

"Helping at my dad's studio," I correct. "The universe doesn't want us to get back together."

"Maybe the universe wants you to bang for old time's sake."

Shivers run down my spine, settle in my breasts and between my thighs.

Sex with Tyler is a terrible idea. Not because I'm not attracted to him. Seeing him strip off his shirt last night to reveal miles of cut pecs and abs covered with swirls of ink... It took everything in me not to melt into the carpet of the fancy hotel suite.

Is that why I didn't want to tell him about Ian—because I was afraid I couldn't handle him if he knew?

I shove the thought down. I can handle Tyler.

All of him.

He's changed over the past two years, and so have I. I'm not a kid anymore, I'm a grown woman with a career and the ability to know what's right for her.

Pen gets up and hugs me again. "Well, I need to go check in with the caterer. It was good to see you. We need to get lunch when we're both back in New York."

"Done."

She waves and vanishes out the door, and I glance at my phone.

I had it set to silent, but the voicemail is lit up, and the number has my good vibes evaporating.

Ian's smooth voice flows out of the speaker when I hit Listen.

"Annie. When you called, I was having breakfast with a couple of colleagues who'll be attending the reading at the end of the summer. Given how soon that is, I need more than a promise to share the book when it's finished. Not only am I hosting this reading, but I'm inviting funders from my own network. It may be your work, but it's my reputation on the line." Pause. "I don't want you to turn what happened between us into an excuse to be unprofessional. What happened with that woman wasn't personal, and it had nothing to do with you and me. Maybe you're too young to understand the difference. Someday, you'll—"

I hang up without listening to the rest.

I'm being unprofessional? You fucked some actress who wanted your connections.

Unreal.

I rub my forehead.

Looking back, I know why I was attracted to Ian. He was older and confident and knew the business. When he advised me, it didn't come off as controlling, it was helpful.

Turned out he liked to advise more than me.

I walked in on him in his apartment with an actress who was, apparently, even more desperate for his mentorship than I was.

Fuck it. I have bigger things to worry about than him.

The café is filling up, and I'm not getting done what I need to here.

I remember the piano in Tyler's office at the studio.

Maybe having the instrument in front of me will help.

On impulse, I buy a second coffee and take that one, plus the one I'm barely halfway through, with me in Haley's car.

Once I get back to the house, I head around to the patio, letting myself in the side door of the studio. Shay's not at the desk, and my hands are too full for signing the visitor's log, so I start down the hall.

The first studio is full, and I can see unfamiliar artists recording inside.

The door to the second is open. I move toward it, pulling up when a figure comes out first.

"Dad!" I exclaim when I nearly bump into him.

He looks as surprised as me. "Annie."

We haven't spoken alone since I've been here.

I guess we're speaking now.

"I was checking on my investment." He cuts a look over his shoulder toward the studio, as if expecting someone to appear, but turns back to me almost as fast.

"Thank you for offering to help with your sister," he says. "We started building the label before Haley got pregnant again, and she didn't want to hold things up."

"Sure."

"You came to watch too?" Shay appears at the end of the hall, bouncing toward me. "They're so good."

She balks when she realizes my dad is there. "Mr. Jamieson, I'm sorry. I didn't see you come in."

"Shay, call me Jax."

"I can't. It's weird."

He frowns, uncomfortable. "Well, get over it."

Dad looks between us then heads for the door without another word.

"God, I fucked that up, didn't I?" she breathes.

"It's fine. My dad doesn't know what to do with candid women who aren't intimidated by him."

"Is that why he married Haley?" Her mouth rounds. "I didn't mean it the way it sounds."

But I'm laughing. "Exactly."

I reach for the door and head inside. Tyler's on the other side of the soundproof glass, arms folded as he listens to the guy that must be my dad's new protégé play his guitar into the mic.

The levels bouncing on the computer screen tell me they're recording something.

My attention is all on Tyler.

He's gorgeous and breathtaking, and parts of me that felt like they were asleep these past months are suddenly awake again.

The kid catches us watching and grins, cocky. His attention still on us, he messes up and Tyler shifts off the wall and jerks the door between us. "Get out," he says to the boy.

"Jax wouldn't—"

"I don't care what Jax would. You have a problem, you can go take it up with him. But I promise you, he gives less fucks than I do."

The kid stalks out the door, kicking a wall on the way.

Tyler emerges next, and he's more frustrated than his charge.

I know the feeling. Since Ian's voicemail, I'm on edge, ready to rip into someone.

Tyler's gaze warms as he spots me. I resist the

urge to run my hands over my clothes before his attention lands on the cup in my hands.

"You brought me a present."

His words strokes over my skin, tugs between my thighs.

"Assuming you take it more cream than coffee, yes. It's a thank you for using the piano in your office. Which isn't technically your office, but I wanted to be polite. I thought you might not even be here given you have that benefit concert in LA tomorrow night."

"I'm leaving in the morning." He hits a few keystrokes on the computer setup, frowning.

"But you're coming back?"

Not that I care. I'm being polite.

"The day after. When'd you use the piano?"

"I'm about to." I take a sip of my coffee and make a face. "The coffee's a bit cold."

"I'll microwave it for you!" Shay grabs the second cup from me and dashes out toward the kitchenette.

When she's gone, I say, "You've got yourself a fan club."

Tyler shakes his head. His mouth curves in a gorgeous half smile as he finishes working on the computer. "The girl knows music. But my heart's unavailable."

My chest caves in a little.

Tyler let me in once. The idea he hasn't let anyone in since feels tragic.

My hand strays to one of the buttons in front of us and Tyler's fingers close over mine. "Don't touch my board."

"You used to like it when I touched your board."

His eyes darken, in arousal or warning or hell, maybe both.

Pen's words come back to me.

Hot rebound sex.

I shove them down.

He swipes my cup before I can protest, inspecting the label. "Double espresso. Someone didn't sleep last night."

I grab it back. "I was up late," I grumble, turning and heading for his office.

Tyler follows. "Not that late."

He closes the door behind me, his shoulder brushing my chest and giving me a hit of that cedar and sunshine scent.

"It was hard to sleep in an unfamiliar bed with an unfamiliar person next to me."

"Bullshit. You know every inch of me."

He looks even better today with messy hair, second-day stubble, a button-down rolled at the sleeves, and dark jeans that hug his hips and legs. Tyler's every bit the rock star, gorgeous enough to send legions swooning, but he has the credibility to back it up.

All of it adds to the frustration from my morning so far.

"Apparently I don't know anything," I blurt before I can stop myself. "I'm young and naïve and can't be trusted with my own feelings, not to mention to finish a musical."

I brush past him to put my coffee cup on his desk before taking a seat on the piano bench, setting out my notebook.

"According to who?" his measured voice comes from right behind me.

I close my eyes. "It doesn't matter. I need to work on this song." I set my fingers on the keys but don't press them. He waits me out as I count my breaths, my mind still spinning, my chest tight with anger and something that I can't name.

"Tyler…" I start before he can leave. "I need to ask you something. Promise you won't read too much into it."

He doesn't answer, so I keep going.

"Tell me you're still attracted to me."

Tyler's heavy exhale is the only response for a long time. His hands find my shoulders, the bare skin revealed by my tank top.

"I'll be attracted to you when we're dead."

Our conversation last night comes back to me in a blur of emotions, past and present and through it all, a kind of need and regret and impatient arousal.

I can't fix the first two, but maybe I can fix the third.

I turn on the bench to find his belt at eye-level. "You said you wished things were different between us at the end." I think of the times we were together, when I was hoping the physicality would bring us closer and it only drove us further apart. "Before you left for tour, you said you owed me."

He lifts my chin to stare into me, through me. "And?"

"And I want to collect."

The inscrutable expression is gone, replaced by heat and arousal.

"You want sex."

"Yes."

He wants a chance to make amends, and I want to prove I can handle myself. That I'm not some child who loses my heart at every turn.

But the look on his face has me second-guessing my idea.

"Tyler! Your coffee's here." Shay bursts through the door, and Tyler steps back. "I'll put it on your desk," she decides, smiling our way.

"Thank you," he answers. "And Shay?"

"Yes?"

"Knock next time."

Her brows pull together. "I did."

"Knock and wait, next time."

"Oh. Sure. Sorry."

With a wave of apology, she ducks out, the door clicking after her.

I exhale hard. "I shouldn't have…"

My words trail off as Tyler steps back in front of me, his fingers threading in my hair.

He's living this as much as I am, his eyes darkening to whiskey mixed with earth.

It's an answer. Adrenaline surges through me as I reach for his jeans, my fingers working on the snap. It's not until the zipper's halfway down that his hand closes over mine.

"Those weren't the terms."

"What do you mean?" My head snaps up.

"I didn't owe you my cock, Six. I owed you my mouth. Take it or leave it."

His words startle me. They're a rough piece of fabric stroking across my skin, making me resist and aware of every inch of him at once.

We've been intimate, sure, but there's so much we haven't done. I realize that now from the way he's looking at me.

"I'll take it."

I may live to regret it, but it's the only answer I have.

Triumph flashes in his eyes. "Good. Spread your legs."

My brows shoot up but I do it, my knees bumping the corners of the bench.

His hand is right there between my thighs, rubbing the seam of denim.

"These shorts look familiar."

I bite my cheek to keep from moaning under his touch. "They're from high school. I stopped short of putting on the Oakwood skirt."

"Too bad. Would've been even easier to do this."

I never thought of him being careful with me before, but when he slips two fingers under the edge of my shorts and beneath my thong, sliding them along my wetness before pressing all the way inside on a long, undeniable stroke, I know it's true.

He's not careful now.

My body squeezes around the invasion, and I gasp as I fall back against the piano, my elbows banging on the keys.

He touches me like that, stroking with those fingers while he circles my clit with his thumb.

Unlike the last times we were together, he's all in this. Present, in this moment.

So am I.

He builds me up with that simple touch. I'm panting by the time he pulls back.

"You know what you want. Say it."

God, he's sexy. All of it makes me stronger, bolder.

"I want your filthy mouth on me."

His chuckle is half groan. "That makes two of us. Take off everything except your thong. Kneel on the bench and brace your elbows on the piano."

There's a hint of something earnest under the command, something that reminds me of last night—how good it felt to be close to him, how he might have something at stake here, too.

It's enough that I don't argue as I shimmy out of the rest of my clothes and his hungry gaze drags over my body.

My nipples are hard buds, and I've soaked through the last remaining item of clothing as I lean over the dark wood, my forearms resting on the cool surface.

Tyler palms my ass. "The show you saw in London. Tell me you fucked yourself to sleep after and wished it was me."

He presses a thick finger inside me and I fall forward, my eyes squeezing shut. Emotions clash in my chest, but I don't want to lie to him. "Yes."

Instead of continuing, he pulls out and plants a kiss on my bare shoulder.

This was a bad idea.

The tension inside me is stronger, bigger, tighter. He's making it worse, not better.

If I ever questioned what happened to the quiet, repressed teenage boy I loved...

He turned into a man. One who won't be denied.

Tyler's fingers comb through my hair. "Wider."

My knees ache from the hard surface but I force them apart another inch. "Happy?"

"Ecstatic. Tell me something. Are you young and naive?" he asks.

I look over my shoulder to meet his gaze. It's hot and hungry and steals my breath.

"No."

I drop my forehead back to the piano and wait.

Tyler drops kisses down my skin, soft but deliberate, one after another. "No, you're fucking not."

He spreads my ass and doesn't hesitate, not even there, until finally, his lips press where I'm hot and wet and aching for him.

"Oh shit, Tyler," I moan.

His scarred hand covers my mouth the next instant. It's all I can do to keep from crying out as his mouth settles between my thighs and he devours me.

Yes.

It might be his mouth on me, but we're equals in giving, in taking. The energy flows between us, tension and relief. We're two musicians improvising together, inspired by one another's actions and reactions.

Nothing in the last two years has felt like this.

Nothing has *ever* felt like this.

My back arches hard, the pressure between the

hand on my mouth and his lips where I'm wet and aching forcing me to coil like a tight, needy spring.

It's only physical.

I repeat it like a mantra, hoping I'll believe it.

"Your legs are shaking," he rasps, his hot breath warming my already-heated skin. "I bet it's been years since you came so hard you forgot your name."

I shudder into his hand.

"Bet it's been even longer since you came so hard you forgot *my* name."

Fuck.

When we had sex before, there was always a sweetness to it. A reverence. As if we were afraid we'd lose each other.

Now it's as if the last shred of protectiveness between us broke.

This isn't sweet.

It's anarchy.

We're not in love.

We're at war.

My first crush, my first love, my first heartbreak... He's back, and he's fucking me with every inch of our baggage.

Tyler builds me up with his lips, his tongue, his fingers.

I'm mindless, my hands sweaty on the piano, to keep my balance or my sanity as I drown in the pleasure.

"Scream if you want," he murmurs against my slick skin, the hand not covering my mouth tracing wet lines down the back of my thigh before gripping possessively around the top. "I've got you."

I don't scream.

But I do come.

In a shaking, sweaty mess of past and present, of bittersweet memories and shocking desire, I break.

Pleasure washes over me in waves, each one rippling further, echoing more faintly, as my cheek sticks to the polished wood.

The tremors leave me smooth and fresh, like sand after the tide goes out.

This was what I needed.

I almost believe it until Tyler leans over me, brushing back my hair to graze his lips across my cheek.

Sweet. Chaste.

Except that if I turned to catch that mouth with mine, I'd taste exactly what he did to me.

I don't remember my name.

But I remember his.

10

Tyler

"Do you have questions about recovery time? The procedure? Anaesthetic?" The surgeon spreads his hands on his desk.

He's for sure taking for granted the range of motion in those fingers, those palms. The sixty-something man might be a doctor, but he's pure California. In living here the past year and a half, I've learned Angelenos can take for granted almost anything.

I shake my head. "I've done it before, at some of the best clinics in the country."

"Well, I like to think we have the best team here at UCLA. You're on the schedule for three weeks from now. I sincerely hope we can get you the results you're looking for in terms of both mobility and pain management."

"Me too."

I leave the clinic and head outside into the sun and get into the waiting car.

It's not my first surgery, but I'm hoping it'll be my last. Beck calls it my obsession, but I think of it as relentless focus.

Since the night a single blade destroyed what I'd worked twenty years to build, I've been aching for the day when I can say I'm back to myself.

I have a few hours before I need to be at the venue for sound check for the benefit concert tonight. I scan the set list, which I'll go over again with my band once I get there.

For the most part, I do vocals and some light chords. The lead guitarist who plays with me is probably good enough to play harder assignments than what I give him, but it makes me envious to hear him do it.

To deal with the monotony of traffic, I go through my email, firing off responses to anything urgent and leaving most of it where it is. After, I open the list of demos Shay sent through from local bands.

I listen to the first, then skip to the next.

Another skip.

I let the third one ride a moment. It's sultry and raw.

I glance at my phone to see what it is.

It's Shay. Not another band, but her.

It's simple, but catchy, and the vocals feel fresh and real.

I file that away as the car reaches my destination, a toy store in La Brea.

Inside, I tell the clerk, "I need a present for a friend's kid. She's four and a half."

"Get her a book on manipulating guys," comes a familiar voice from behind me before the clerk can respond. "It must be some secret coming-of-age thing, because all chicks seem to know it by the time they're twelve."

I turn toward Beck and grin, clapping him on the back. He looks every part the actor in jeans, boots, and a white T-shirt. His aviators are shoved back on his head.

"Thanks for meeting me," I say. "Tell me you haven't burned down the apartment yet."

"Nah, but you might want to stay in it sometime."

I shake my head. The two-bedroom place we share is way bigger than the New York apartment we had until I left on tour and that Beck kept until graduation.

"I'm heading out again in a couple of days. I made a deal to help Jax out with his new studio." I huff out a breath as I scan the shelves for a gift for Sophie.

"You're supposed to be in *your* studio. Recording at *your* label," he reminds me. "The one who pays *your* income, which covers half of *our* rent."

"Thank you for that lesson in pronouns. I have three weeks until my surgery so I'm taking a vacation."

I pick up a puzzle. Maybe Sophie's into these. Something with fish or birds, exotic ones she wouldn't see in Dallas.

"A vacation with Annie Jamieson. I saw your post the other night. You might not've tagged her, but you're so busted."

"Nothing to bust. We hung out."

But my abs clench under my shirt at the sound of her name.

The purple dump truck on the shelf triggers my memory that Sophie's into things with wheels. I lift it off the shelf as Beck grins. "I bet you did."

I cut him a look, but my retort dies on my lips. My roommate's the one person other than Annie and Jax who can see through my bullshit.

Still, I'm not about to tell him I lost control the moment she peered up at me with those doe eyes wanting to collect on what I owed her.

Turned out I was on the receiving end of something priceless.

I'm man enough to admit that the best moments of my life have been spent holding that woman.

And yesterday, she was wild. From the second I found her under those tight shorts, soaked and squirming, it was a breakneck descent into madness.

I wanted nothing more than to free my swollen cock and sink into her as far as I'd go, to see her beautiful body arch and writhe on that dark wood backdrop.

But I spent the last two years knowing Annie and I ended because she got over me first.

Still, the way she looked at me, the way she asked me for it...

It took everything in me to remember we're not together.

Beck squeezes a stuffed toy hard enough it squeaks. "I'm relieved to hear it's nothing serious. Because you were fucked up after it ended. You *both* were."

I round on him, boxing him in against the shelf. "Go on."

"She couldn't go with you, and you couldn't stay. Someone had to be the bad guy. Otherwise, you wouldn't have moved on—not just from her, with your life."

Hearing it spelled out is bringing up old feelings.

Not even the bitterness of leaving, but the things it's taken me two years to appreciate.

How fucking incredible she is.

How much I loved her.

How much she loved *me*.

"You didn't tell me she was seeing someone," I say. "Did you think I'd be jealous?"

"Did I think you'd look like you're looking right now? Yes."

"But they broke up," I say, pouncing.

He frowns. "I heard. He's some big producer type. And—please use this for good, and not evil—apparently he cheated on her. A casting couch situation with some actress." Beck reads the disbelief on my face. "Fucking tool, yeah. You know our girl has always had some issues believing she was enough. With all she's accomplished, I hope she sees it and never gives the guy another look."

I turn that over as I start toward the cash register, dump truck in tow.

I hope to hell she didn't fall for Ian because she thought she needed him. The fact that he hurt her makes me want to crush the only good fist I have left into his face.

But thinking of the ex has a dark thought occurring to me.

I liked the idea she wanted me yesterday, wanted another shot at how we'd ended things.

Was he the reason she was questioning herself in the first place?

I'm not stupid enough to think what happened between us was some kind of a sign—we've both moved on, I've got an album to make and she's finishing a show—but fuck it, I need to know.

"Tyler." Zeke walks into my dressing room after sound check, and I shift back in my chair.

The guys from the band are around me, talking amongst themselves, but when he enters, they nod deferentially before ducking out into the hall to make themselves scarce.

The exec drops onto the arm of the couch. "You've been posting on social."

"You proud?" I drawl.

"The venue you tagged is in Dallas." He frowns. "There's a strict competition clause in your contract. You can't record for any other label."

"I was visiting an old friend. Remember, I'm on the first vacation I've had in two years. Once I get through this surgery, I'll be back in the studio to finish the album."

"You know your career has nothing to do with your hand."

I shift back in my seat, a humorless smile pulling across my face. "You're saying that day Jax and I went to your house senior year, if I hadn't been able to play, you still would've offered me a deal."

He narrows his gaze. "Two hundred years ago,

men figured out how to make music with machines. The player piano. The music box. Everyday people could have music when they wanted—accurate, predictable, perfect.

"Being proficient in playing doesn't make you a good musician. Being proficient in feeling—in believing what you're doing so much it makes someone listening, someone watching, connect with it—that's what it's fucking about.

"That's what I saw in you that day. A quiet, gives-zero-shits kid who came alive the second he picked up a guitar."

His words are unsettling, though I'm saved examining them too closely when my phone buzzes with an incoming call from Annie.

"Regardless of the outcome of your procedure, I expect you back in studio the next week or you'll be paying for missed time out of your royalties," Zeke tosses as he heads for the door.

"Always a pleasure."

Zeke and I have always had a rocky relationship, but my relentless focus on being the best I can clashes with his "make money first" approach."

He disappears down the hall and I go back to my phone, hitting Accept.

"Everything okay?" I answer, concerned.

"Yes. Fine," Annie says, a little breathless. "I just called to say good luck tonight."

I'm still on edge from Zeke's threat, my hand tightening on the phone.

I haven't spoken to her since yesterday in the studio, and the sound of her voice has every part of me tightening as I remember the way she fell apart under my hands and my mouth.

But despite my physical response to her now, I can't help thinking of all the times she didn't call to wish me good luck when I was on tour. The times I didn't text her because I knew she was busy.

She's calling now.

Which means nothing. Tell her goodnight. Get moving.

"How was your day?" I ask instead, shifting out of the chair and leaning over the bureau, pressing my bad hand on the surface. The fingers won't straighten all the way.

"Less exciting than yours. Took Sophie to daycare. Met Pen for coffee before she headed back to New York. Worked on the musical. Went for a swim. With the bathing suit this time," she adds lightly.

I turn over my hand and inspect the tangle of black vines and thorns and roses, the white lines beneath. Layers upon layers of ink and scars, like the layers of lies and feelings and decisions that litter our past.

I should be hanging up, both to get on with my

prep and because talking to her like this feels too good, too much like something I could look forward to.

"I was listening to a demo Shay sent in the car today," I hear myself say. "She's good. I'd love to cut the punk loose and put Shay in the studio instead."

"Then do it."

Her direct reply takes me by surprise. "This isn't my fight. It's not my music."

"Diving into someone else's mess can be the best way to get out of your own. Maybe you need something bigger than yourself to believe in."

My bassist sticks his head in the doorway, calling my name and jerking his head toward the stage.

I take a last look in the mirror at my stage getup, the makeup, the hair—all done by professionals to craft a man who looks like me but isn't quite.

"Tell me yesterday wasn't you trying to fuck your ex out of your head."

My blunt words have her pausing. But there's a cord of strength in her voice when she responds. "I think I needed to feel alive in a way I haven't felt in a long time. I wanted to feel in control, which I know is a weird way to think of what happened, but it's true."

Maybe I haven't been alive these past two years despite the crowds and the music and pressing past every challenge that's been leveled at me.

Maybe I didn't feel in control until I had her

heated skin under my lips, her hot breath on my hand, her tight body squeezing me when she broke apart.

When I answered her call, I wanted to prove my heart doesn't beat for her.

But now, it's hammering harder than ever.

"You are the most alive person I've ever met," I say. "I saw your show in New York four times. I couldn't see opening night off-Broadway because we had a gig in Colorado. But the second night, I flew in. And your first night on Broadway. I even saw it once without you in it, because there was something I suspected but wanted to know for sure."

I block out the noises from the backstage crew, the chatter and footsteps in the hall, until all I hear is her soft breathing. "What's that?"

"It was better with you."

Everything's better with you.

11

———

Annie

This morning, there's no alarm to wake me to start working.

There's no screaming from downstairs, no sound of Sophie shrieking, no daycare.

But I'm awake and warm and itchy.

I've been at Dad and Haley's for four days. The first couple of nights, I slept through without waking. Since Tyler left for LA, though, I've been restless and turned on.

I still haven't found the breakthrough I need with my final song, and I know Ian's breathing down my neck. Soon Miranda will be, too.

So, this morning, I give myself this one thing.

I slide a hand down the front of my pajamas, where I'm already wet.

It's a bad idea to fantasize about a man you can't have.

I didn't let myself do it when we were apart, save for a couple of times when I gave myself a pass on account of being too tipsy to regulate my fantasizing or having a really brutal day of rehearsing or, once, when he did a spread for this magazine where I swear he was looking right at me and seeing every dirty thought I've ever had about him—when we were together and since.

A few sweaty minutes in the studio—no matter how earth-shattering—doesn't change anything.

What about you calling him before his show?

I did it to prove that all the months he was on the road, I hadn't held him at a distance because I wanted him out of my life.

But it didn't play out the way I expected.

It was better with you.

It sounded as if he didn't only mean the show. I wanted him to mean that.

But I can't fall for Tyler Adams again.

My heart wouldn't survive it.

When he comes back later today, there'll be no more longing looks, no more flirty winks, and definitely no more thinking about how the only thing terrible about having his tongue in me was that it wasn't his cock.

As a consolation prize, I give myself the best solo orgasm I've had in years.

The release seems to shake loose a few ideas, and when I get out of the shower, I jot down half a page of notes in the notebook on my desk.

Then I dress and go downstairs to grab coffee with Haley, who's sitting on a chair with her feet on another.

"You okay?" I ask.

"Fine. Your dad was hoping to talk to you. He's staining the gazebo. I swear he went out and made millions of dollars so he could live like he had his own home reno show."

"You love it."

She grins. "Yeah, I do."

I turn that over as I go to find him.

I weave through the manicured lawns on the other side of the house, around a grove of trees.

Sophie's playing with her trucks in the grass a dozen feet away from the gazebo my dad built for Haley with his band's help.

"Annie! Play trucks with me. This one's Boom. And that's Mice."

"Mouse?" I ask.

"Mice."

"She named it after Mace," Dad weighs in from where he's painting one of the beams, sweat dripping down his face.

"Annie, you'd be a red truck."

"Perfect." My gaze drifts back to my dad. "Haley could use some love." My dad cocks a brow, and I shudder. "Not like that. Just... whatever, you do you."

I take in the gazebo, its graceful beams and arches. "Didn't you just build that five years ago?"

"People think building things takes effort. But maintaining them is harder." He takes a seat on the top step, balancing the brush on the edge. "When something's in my care, I keep it a certain way. Maybe it's the right way, and maybe it's not. But I can't apologize for doing things the best I know how."

"Can you apologize for hurting the people you love?"

He doesn't answer, but I see the strain in the tight lines of his face.

"There's something I need to say to you," he goes on at last, and I hold my breath.

This is it. An apology.

"The scholarship you got at Vanier that covered the rest of your tuition and living expenses through graduation. That was me."

I stiffen. "What are you talking about? I told you I didn't need your help."

"And I didn't accept that."

My mouth works. "All you had to do was say you were wrong. Instead you had to control the situation again and manipulate me into taking your money."

He leans forward, bracing his elbows on his knees. "That's not what it was."

"No?"

His groan has Sophie looking up over her trucks, her curious gaze cutting between us.

"I don't want your money. I mean, it helped," I concede, shoving a hand through my hair. "I can't pretend it didn't. But all I ever wanted was for you to respect me. To see me as an equal."

"You're not equal to *anything*. You're my child. You will always mean more to me than anything in this world has a right to mean."

My throat swells at the emotion in his words. "I just want you to know that I can handle myself. That you'd bet on me if I wasn't your child. I want you to think I've grown into the kind of person you'd believe in."

I hold out a hand for the paint brush. "Go hang with Haley. I'll finish it."

His gaze finds mine, surprised. "And watch your sister?"

I lower my voice. "I've pulled together changes from a whole host of writers. I can handle a four-year-old and a paint brush."

My dad looks as if he's about to say something, but in the end, he hands me the brush.

After finishing up at the gazebo, I scrounge some lunch for me and Sophie before taking a call with Miranda while my sister plays.

We talk about the work, catch up on Ian. I let her know he's pushing me.

"I emailed and told him I'd send him what we have next week."

"What did he say?"

I huff out a breath. "Nothing, yet. But I have to go," I say to my writing partner as I look up to see Sophie climbing on the windowsill and jumping on the seat.

"I know you're dealing with family issues, but we need to finish that song."

"I will."

If my voice has an edge, it's in response to the urgency in hers. "I have a version, Miranda. And it's good. But it's not right."

"You have good instincts. If there's something more you can get from it, I trust you to try."

"Thank you. I know it's your dream to co-write a show from the beginning. We'll make it work."

What happened with Ian was my mistake, not hers, and I'll make sure it doesn't hurt us.

After hanging up, I get Sophie off the windowsill.

"I want to swim," she decides, peering up at me.

"Okay. But after, we need some quiet play time so I can work."

I get her changed, and she insists on bringing the trucks with her.

My gaze cuts toward the hedges and the parking lot beyond.

"That's Tyler's car," Sophie informs me.

"Yes, it is." His flight was supposed to get back from LA around noon, and I chastise myself for being so obvious a toddler could figure it out as I usher her toward the pool.

"Why're you so into trucks?" I ask as she's clinging to the ladder, her water wings keeping her afloat.

"They get things done. Like Mommy."

I laugh. "Not Daddy?"

She wrinkles her nose. "No. Daddy makes messes. Mommy cleans them up."

"That's true."

I coax her off the ladder, stabilizing her with my hands as she kicks wildly.

"Where's your Mommy?" she pants.

Her question catches me off-guard, and I stare at her freckled little face. Apparently Dad and Haley have had this conversation with her—or at least part of it. "Um. I'm not sure."

"Why not?"

"Because she lives somewhere else. I haven't really talked to her." Not since the letter she sent me.

"Why not?"

I lift my feet from the shallow bottom, sculling with my hands. "Because she's not really part of my life right now."

"Do you think she gets things done or makes messes?"

"I don't know, Soph. I guess I always picture her getting things done. Like your Mommy." I shake my head. "Come on. We should get out, or we'll turn into prunes."

We get out, and I help her get the water wings off.

She tosses them on the patio with a scrunched-up face. "I hate those."

"Then why'd you want to swim?"

Sophie peers up at me, squinting against the sun as she grins. "Because you like it."

She says it like it's obvious, and my heart melts.

"You will always mean more to me than anything in this world has a right to mean."

I swallow as I think of my dad's words.

I can't pretend I know how hard it would be to have kids, how they test your patience. But the way she's looking at me, I know there's nothing I wouldn't do for her.

"Stay put," I tell Sophie, "I need to get towels."

She heads for her trucks under one of the patio chairs while I go to the cabana on the other side of the patio.

The top shelf is empty, but there should be extras

below. I'm rummaging around inside and finally spot a stash tucked behind some other supplies when I hear a splash behind me.

"Sophie?" I call over my shoulder, grabbing two towels.

No answer.

My veins turn to ice.

I whirl and bolt from the cabana, my gaze scanning the patio where she was a moment ago.

No sign of her.

Until I spot her form beneath the surface of the pool.

"Sophie!" I scream.

I need to get to her. I know it in my mind, but my legs won't cooperate.

My throat tightens, every part of me numb.

Go. Go. Fucking go.

Suddenly I do, springing toward the pool.

But in the same moment, a form leaps over the fence from the direction of the studio and dives into the pool headfirst.

My head thuds dully and my nails dig into my palms as Tyler cuts through the water.

It feels like a lifetime before he emerges with Sophie, who's coughing. He lifts her out and sets her on the side of the pool before hefting himself out, his jeans, T-shirt, and jacket soaked and his hair black and dripping.

I race toward them, my arms wrapping around her wet form. "Oh my God. Are you okay?"

I pull back to look in her pale face. She's breathing, though blinking and disoriented.

When her coughing relents, she mumbles. "My red sister truck was in the pool."

I look over the edge to see the red truck on the bottom. My stomach plummets as I wrap one of the towels still clutched in my hands around her.

Tyler's voice is low, shaken. "I'll get her toy."

He wrenches off his drenched jacket, but before he can shift away, I clamp a hand around his wrist. I can't stand the thought of him going anywhere right now. "No."

"Annie, I'm soaked," he protests.

After a moment, his arms go around both of us. I don't give a shit about his wet clothes. I need him here.

"Are *you* okay?" Tyler murmurs.

I shake my head. "I couldn't move," I whisper. "I panicked, and I couldn't do anything and…"

The backs of my eyes burn as my gaze drops to his hand, scarred and tattooed.

His face fills with understanding and an emotion I can't name.

"It's okay, Six. It wasn't your fault."

Sophie squirms, and I shudder out a breath.

"Let's go inside and make a snack. How do Rice Krispies squares sound?"

"I don't like squares. Can we make them circles?"

Tyler's face is pale, but his lips curve up in a ghost of a smile.

"Yeah, we can make them circles," I hear myself say before dropping Tyler's hand and rising. "You come inside too," I tell him.

***

"It's so sticky." Sophie's digging into her first circle with fascination—I used a cookie cutter to make them—when Tyler comes in, his hair damp from the shower in the guest bathroom.

He's dressed in a black T-shirt of my dad's and jeans an inch too short, but he still looks handsome as ever.

"I bet this is what you came back from LA for," I tease, trying to keep it light. "Lifeguard duty."

He steps closer, scanning my form. I'm still in my bathing suit, a towel wrapped over it. "You must be cold. I can watch Sophie if you want to shower."

"Thanks. But I don't want to let her out of my sight."

I wrap my arms around myself and cut a look towards my sister.

She's turning the pages of a picture book, happily dressed in pajamas in the middle of the day.

A week ago, I was barely part of this family. Now, it's all I can think about.

This family and him. The boy who's always been in me, with me.

Suddenly, I can't hold the feelings in anymore.

"Tyler." The moment I look back toward him, those dark eyes are on me. "How do you know when something's over? Is it when the world tells you it is? When you decide it?"

He's silent, but I can see the wheels turn behind his eyes.

"I know when you went on tour," I go on, "things were messed up. But there was never a time I didn't want you," I tell him. "You didn't seem to think you were whole anymore, and I hated that I had contributed to that."

His expression fills with anguish as he steps closer, his body a breath away. "Annie, none of it was your fault. You have to know that."

Despite my vows to keep my distance, I can't keep from reaching my arms around his neck to play with the damp hair that curls at his collar. My gaze runs over his chest, the hard lines under his shirt—not because I'm checking him out, though his closeness is making me ache for his touch, but because I can't meet his gaze.

"In acting class my final term at Vanier, we had to prep monologues about our heroes. Elle talked about her mom. Some people chose public figures. I chose you."

He stiffens under me, and I force my eyes up to his because I need to see his face. His expression is filled with longing and something I'm afraid to name.

I'm trapped in his stare, the tension twisting me, wringing me out like one of the wet towels by the pool.

"You will always be my hero, Tyler Adams. The way you try, the way you fight no matter what life sends your way... you are everything I want to be, and it has nothing to do with your music and everything to do with who you are in here."

My hand covers his heart, his chest warm through the borrowed T-shirt.

"Everyone okay?" Haley asks as she and my dad enter the room.

We step apart, but not before Haley's gaze turns knowing and my dad eyes us suspiciously. "Yeah. Everyone's good."

A distinctive ringtone from my phone on the coffee table has me stiffening in his arms.

"What is it?" Tyler asks.

I know before I answer. "Real life."

12

Annie

"You're not going back to New York for your ex," Tyler states from behind me as I throw my makeup and toiletries into the tiny suitcase on my bed.

"It's work," I insist. "I've been here a week, and even though I told my collaborators what's going on, they need assurances. Especially Ian, because he's central to the funding of this entire venture."

The past two days, we've been hanging out around the house and the studio. I think he's worried about me since Sophie fell into the pool, waiting for me to fall apart.

I won't, but I like having an excuse to spend time with him.

Once I've got my essentials into my bag, I zip the thing closed and drop onto the bed.

Tyler crosses to the edge of the bed, leaning over to stare down at me with broody eyes.

"I don't trust him. He's an asshole."

"Ian?" I laugh. "How do you know?"

"Beck—"

"Beck told you?" I shift up on my elbows. "When did you talk to Beck about me?"

I think he's going to deny it, but he only tugs on his hair. "In LA. I hate that someone hurt you."

My chest twinges. "You're a grown man now. You going to beat him up for me?"

"If you want."

The earnestness in his voice makes me ache.

I shut my eyes, not against him, but against the feelings.

I can't have them. Not because I don't think he feels something too, but because giving into them is dangerous.

I nearly lost myself when I had to let Tyler go the last time. It would break me if I had to do it again.

I feel him shift over me, the bed denting under his weight.

I blink my eyes open to see him hovering inches away, studying me from under his thick, dark lashes. Every nerve in me tingles with anticipation.

Not only between my thighs, but *everywhere*.

"I need to get to the airport," I say, my voice breathy.

Neither of us moves.

The past few days with him, the familiarity creeps in everywhere—the inside jokes, the teasing. He'll smile or say something so classic deadpan Tyler that I have to remind myself we're not dating.

Sometimes, I'm not sure I want to remind myself we're not dating.

He always made me feel things no other guy could, but now he's making me feel things I didn't know I was capable of.

Physically. Emotionally.

And that's the problem.

I care about Tyler more than I should, more than it's safe to care.

But I shove that aside because even if he feels it too, I can't give in.

We're ships passing, him and me. Even if we can find common ground, how long can it last—a day? A week?

The only thing we have in common is that neither of us belongs here, and neither of us can stay.

Even if we could, we've never been able to stay together for an extended period of time without spinning out. Tyler won't let me in—truly, deeply let me in—to see his hurt. I can't be with someone who'd choose to bear his wounds alone.

"You can leave after you kiss me," he says.

My fingers find his forearms, digging in. His firm lips are inches away.

I want them on me.

"No," I whisper. "Because if I kiss you, I can't pretend we're friends right now."

"As opposed to what?"

We stare each other down.

That I never stopped loving you.

That I'm falling for you again.

Tyler shifts back, his face unreadable.

I get out from beneath him before I change my mind.

"When'd you get the ink on your hand?" I ask over my shoulder as I grab the hair dryer I nearly forgot from my bathroom.

"In between shows on tour. I wanted to cover up something ugly with something beautiful."

When I return from the bathroom, he's reclined on the bed.

I tuck the dryer in the front pocket of my bag before straightening.

"You're beautiful, Tyler. You will always be beautiful."

I reach for his scarred hand and lift it to my lips.

His skin is rough and warm, and I want more of him—all of him.

"Whatever's between us now..." I take a long

breath. "It can't stop me from going to New York. And neither can you."

He pulls his hand back and rises from the bed, his clothes tugging across the strong, deliberate lines of his body. "I know. I'll take your bag down to the car."

After my flight arrives at La Guardia, I stop by my apartment to drop my things and change. It feels strange to be back after only a week away. It's my space, filled with things Elle and I love, but suddenly I'm noticing what isn't here—big, bright windows everywhere letting in natural light, the sound of Sophie's feet thudding on the carpet as she tears into a room or out of it.

Elle texted to say she's working all weekend, hustling out some gigs with a new agent, and might not be back tonight.

In my tiny room, I change into a fitted red dress that ends partway down my thighs. The neck is a V, and I open my jewelry box to search for a chain to wear with it.

My gaze lands on one in particular, and my stomach knots.

It's still there, curled into one of the compartments, the rings preserved in time like the rose.

My fingers itch, and I think how easy it would be to slip it over my head.

In the end, I can't decide on another necklace, so I go without one.

Ian wanted to meet at my apartment, but I told him we'd meet at a restaurant. I should've known something was up when he gave me the location. It's the hottest place in town, inside a shiny, recently reopened Midtown hotel. It's glass and minimalist elegance. The sky-high ceilings and white space scream money, as they're meant to.

Ian's waiting at a prime table when I arrive.

My ex is the opposite of Tyler, though I never realized it until now. He's quick with a smile, the life of a party, grew up with everything handed to him. His father's in real estate; his mother in the arts. He did a combination of things, running galleries, but his real interest is in performance arts.

Ian wears a suit like a skin, as if he fell out of bed and slid effortlessly into the tailored wool.

"Annie. You look gorgeous," Ian says easily as I cross to him.

I smooth a hand down my dress. The nude open-toe heels were the perfect addition for a business dinner somewhere fancy.

I put the outfit on feeling as if I was going into a negotiation, but the way he's looking at me, he's not thinking of fighting.

Ian steps close, hands resting on my bare arms. I turn my cheek so his kiss lands there, and I step out of his arms smoothly as the waiter holds my chair.

"Thank you for booking the restaurant. I'm glad we have an opportunity to talk business."

"Thank you for coming. Let's order first." He gets steak, and I order salmon. Once the waiter disappears, Ian grins. "Tell me what you've been up to with your family in Dallas. I hope I didn't drag you away."

A glass of wine appears without my ordering it, and I take a sip, grateful. "My family is fine, thank you. I hope yours is too."

"You know my mom. It's the middle of fundraising season, so she's in her element."

I smile tightly. "The show's nearly completed. As you know, I'm working on the lyrics for the last couple of songs. Honestly, I hoped it'd come faster. But they're the most important."

Ian's smile doesn't waver. "Annie, I know we planned to more formally discuss my involvement in funding after the reading next month." The event is a tradition, taking place at Ian's apartment, involving half a dozen actors plus the writing team and a host of prospective funders from Manhattan's elite circles. "But I think we can move sooner."

My heart kicks in my chest. "Really? You never sign on to a project until all the pieces are in place and you have a chance to discuss it with people you trust."

"But this is your project." He lifts his glass in a toast. "If I commit first, getting the rest of the funders lined up will be simple. We can get this where it needs to be. Together."

Suspicion crawls up my spine. "What exactly does that mean?"

"It means we'll meet every few days while you're finishing the book. In New York, obviously. I'd like to be on top of my investment."

"With Miranda."

Ian hesitates. "I don't see the need to use her unnecessarily."

There it is. I shift in my seat as he continues.

"I know how shows are developed. I'm experienced, and you're talented. Together, we make a good team."

I shiver as I feel his leg brush mine under the table.

Our meals come, and he digs in immediately, but I can't.

"We're not getting back together, Ian."

He stops chewing halfway through a bite, brows lifting on his handsome face. After he swallows, he plasters on a smile I've seen a thousand times. "You're getting emotional. Reading something into this that isn't there."

"I didn't read into the part where I walked in on you fucking an eighteen-year-old actress on your couch."

When I rise, he's out of his seat too, reaching for me. "Hey. Come on."

His hand grips my arm. I stare at that hand until he releases me.

"This isn't about me," he bites out. "It's about *him*."

"I'm not seeing anyone." Except as I say the words, they don't feel entirely true.

"Maybe you never touched another man while we were together. But you held back. It's my job to see the beauty in things. That's what attracted me to you. On stage, you're this wild thing. Full of emotion and passion, unrestrained. But you were never that woman with me."

I'm shaking my head, but he continues.

"At first I thought I wasn't doing the right things to bring it out of you." He cocks his head, studying me in a way I can't deny him. "But that was a lie. Which meant you were saving it for something else. Someone else."

His words trip me because he's never said them before, not while we were together or after we broke up.

"There's always a silver lining to these situations," he continues. "I believe in your voice, and I have all the connections in the Manhattan arts community. I can make it easy for you to get this show produced. Or"—he adjusts the cuffs on his jacket—"I can make it difficult."

Cold washes over me at his barely veiled threat.

I know I could work with him, turn away his advances. I trust myself, and I know he has the money and connections to make my dream a reality.

I fold my napkin and set it on the table next to my plate.

"You're right, Ian. There is a silver lining."

His eyes soften, as if he knows I'm seeing reason.

"What is this wine?" I ask him.

Ian balks a moment, surprised, but tells me.

I nod. "It's great." I make a note to get Pen a bottle as I lift my glass to him before taking a long sip, letting the flavors play over my tongue. "But dinner was a mistake."

He glances around, as if suddenly unsure of what's happening.

"You can take your funding and your contacts and your threats and go fuck yourself. Yourself and every other person in Manhattan if you like. But you won't be fucking me, in bed or out of it."

I drain the last sip of wine before setting the glass back on the table.

"Enjoy the rest of your evening." I turn on my heel and head out toward the front of the restaurant.

I'm pissed—pissed at his nerve, even if I shouldn't be surprised by it.

I don't regret what I did, but I can't shake the feeling that it could cost me.

Ian's not bluffing. He has the contacts to make my life easier or harder.

I'll deal with it. I've dealt with everything else that's come my way. This project is too important to go down because of him.

I pass the separate bar area of the hotel flanked by floor-to-ceiling glass windows and chrome chandeliers. My gaze catches on a man in a black sport coat and jeans at the bar.

My steps slow and I change directions, cutting a straight path for him. "What are you doing here?" I ask as I pull up next to him.

Tyler turns at the sound of my voice.

His gaze drops down my body, eyes warming with appreciation. "I couldn't stop you from coming. But I could come with you."

He turns a crystal lowball glass filled with ice and clear liquid in one hand, eyes crinkling with satisfaction and something like amusement.

A moment ago, all I wanted was to get out of this restaurant, but his presence is like an escape valve, a life preserver.

"How's dinner?" he goes on as if this is a completely normal situation.

"Well." I shift in next to him at the bar and drum my fingers on the surface. "I found an amazing red wine."

I tell him the name, and he nods to the bartender for two glasses.

"And the company?" Tyler presses as he turns back to me, his gaze more serious.

"It's rapidly improving."

I lift the wine and hold it out to him in a toast. He grins as he clinks his glass lightly with mine, and my heart kicks in my chest.

The wine tastes delicious on my tongue, comfort down my throat.

"I'm guessing the fact that you're here instead of with him doesn't bode well for your show."

"It does not," I concede. "But I will figure it out. I always do."

"Yes, you do. And I have a gift for you."

I'm intrigued even before he pushes a paper bag down the bar.

"Is it millions of dollars?" I quip.

"Better."

I open it and peer inside, the scent of potatoes and oil making my stomach growl. "Oh my God. Cheese fries."

"From the diner near that comedy club we used to like. I watched you through the glass for the last ten minutes," he admits. "Didn't see you pick up your fork once."

Tyler's not trying to touch me, to grab me, to make me do anything or be anything. He's just here, bringing me five-dollar French fries in a five-star hotel.

God, I missed my friend.

I know my heart was broken when we parted ways, when I chose both our dreams over our future together, but I downplayed how much it hurt not to have this—the calm, dryly funny, quietly charming guy I've adored since before I knew what charm was.

We eat every last fry and talk about everything. Tyler and Beck's life in LA. Elle's new show and whether she and her agent have something going on. How I'm stuck on the last few verses of the most important song for this musical. The fact that he got Shay into the studio before coming to New York and was rewarded by something better than he could've imagined.

"I told your dad I wanted to swap his dumbass kid for Shay."

I grin. "How'd that go over?"

"Not great."

It's kind of nice to know I'm not the only person who argues with him.

I gaze past Tyler at the sparkling people and tables.

A couple of tables still cut looks at us, one discreetly trying to take pictures.

"We're going to be on the internet in thirty minutes, if we're not already," I murmur.

Tyler reaches for the wine glass. "Do you care? Because I don't."

I shake my head, smiling as he drinks. The way he fills out his unfussy jacket is a tailor's wet dream. The dark, messy hair makes me itch to run my hands through it.

Ian's words come back.

You're saving yourself for someone.

I was.

Maybe I still am.

"For an unavailable guy, you're acting pretty available," I comment after we've finished the bottle of wine and I've won rock paper scissors for the last stub of a fry in the bottom of the greasy paper box.

Tyler frowns, confused. "What do you mean?"

"When I said Shay had a crush on you," I remind him, "you said she didn't have a shot because you're unavailable."

Understanding dawns. The fact that he doesn't argue with me has my stomach sinking.

"Please tell me you're not seeing someone. That there's not some woman who thinks she's yours."

The idea is unbearable.

Tyler pulls his bottom lip between his teeth. "No," he says at last. "I'm not seeing anyone."

Relief washes over me, and I can breathe again. But the fear spiking through me a moment ago also reminds me how only a few days with him has me wanting things I have no business wanting with him.

Tyler swipes the bill for the drinks before I can, but the laughter's faded from his eyes, replaced by something serious and maybe even sad. "Let me drive you home."

***

"You got quiet," Tyler observes in the town car as we cruise through the city toward my apartment.

The lights penetrate the back windows, creating strips of illumination that run over his body and mine.

"There's not enough quiet in the world." I lean my head on his shoulder, and Tyler huffs out a breath.

When we pull up in front of the building, I have to force my legs out of the car because I don't want it to end.

"Walk me to my door?" I say on impulse.

He shifts out of the car after me, a dark presence at my side. Like a dog who looks menacing or unapproachable to a stranger, he's the comfort no one will ever understand.

They don't have to.

In the hall outside my apartment, I fish my keys out of my bag. There's a note on the door from Elle.

If you're coming home with NT, I'm going to kill you.

Tyler lifts the note off the door, frowning. "Who's NT?"

"She means Ian. It's an inside joke." I take the note, crumpling it into a ball. My stomach tightens as I think about what the nickname means.

"Annie." Tyler steps between the door and me before I can slide the key into the lock. "Why did you date him?"

I've asked myself the same question so many times these past few days.

"I thought he was what I wanted. He didn't look at me like I was crazy when I told him about my dreams. Though I guess he liked it because he could take advantage."

"I have always believed in you."

I nod. "I know. That's the other reason I was drawn to him."

"Why?"

"Because he was safe. Because I didn't love him the way I loved you."

Tyler's body relaxes, and I peer up into his face.

There's urgency that wasn't there at the hotel, but he's holding back.

"Say it," I demand. "Whatever it is that has you looking all broody after I thought we had a good time."

He captures my wrist, and I suck in a startled little breath as he strokes his thumb across my skin. The electricity between us that was content to sit back over dinner and drinks springs to life once again.

Tyler turns my hand and skims his thumb across the lines in my palm, so different from the lines on his. "The reason I'm unavailable isn't because I'm seeing someone else."

When his gaze meets mine, the emotion in his eyes hits me square in the chest. "It's because my heart has always been yours."

13

Tyler

I didn't come to New York to tell Annie Jamieson I love her. I came because I couldn't let her go off to see some dickhead who hurt her without having backup. I know I've been that dickhead, but I won't be him this time.

She's flushed in the hall lights, a warm, lush shade that makes me want to kiss her everywhere. I want to capture her with my hands, my mind, so I can have her like this whenever I want.

"My heart has been yours since you walked into the pool house to steal my towel senior year at Oakwood," I continue.

Annie's lips part, those amber eyes blinking as she sucks in a slow breath.

If she tells me to leave, I will. I'll walk out of here

and never come back, never insert myself into her life again when she hasn't asked for it.

Instead, she holds out a hand. "Give me your phone."

I take it out, unlocking it for her.

She opens my contacts and hits a number, telling the driver downstairs he can leave.

Her meaning sinks in, and my body gets heavy—hard.

I turn us so it's her back against the door, my hips colliding with hers. She doesn't resist, doesn't do anything but angle her face up to mine.

"Listen to me." I plant my hand on the wall next to her head instead of threading it into her hair like I want to. "If this is about blowing off steam, about you being pissed at your ex or the world, I can be your friend. But I won't fuck you tonight."

Confusion clouds her expression. "But you said—"

"I know what I said," I interrupt. My breath is too shallow for the words I need to say, but I say them anyway. "It's not enough to know you're not his, Annie. I need to know you're mine."

The words settle between us.

She weighs them as if each is worthy of its own assessment.

It's what I wanted, for her to take me seriously,

but Annie thinks on those words for so fucking long it's going to break me.

"Tyler…"

Her arms wind around my neck, and she holds me tighter, hugging me with every ounce of strength in her. I breathe her in, but every part of me knows she's going to say something I don't want to hear.

"You're right. I did find myself in New York. I've learned how to be tough. How to take care of myself and go after my dreams. I wouldn't have become that person without everything that happened, and a lot of it is thanks to you.

"I'm not sure I can give my heart to you the way you're asking. But," she continues before I can pull away, "I loved the boy you were then. I love the man you are now."

I understand everything she's saying. It's more than I had a right to hope for.

I have her as much as anyone can.

"I tried to cut you out, Annie. I wanted to forget you but I couldn't. You're so deep inside me I can't get you out. I never touched another woman on tour. When you're close, there's no air. But when you're gone… I don't care if I breathe again."

Her gaze searches mine as if she's trying to figure a way through this moment.

In my life, I've started taking the things I want,

stopped making apologies for it. Now… I wait. For the first time in two fucking years, I wait.

Her hands slide down my chest and rest there. She inches forward, closing the distance between us.

She's close enough I can taste her slow exhale, smell her shampoo.

Her tongue darts out to wet her lips, and I want to do it for her.

I haven't kissed her in two years, and I know it's because she's been holding back.

The moment she decides, my heart stops.

When Annie's lips brush mine, it's honest and vulnerable. It's a plea. It's a promise. It's all the words and all the actions ever invented rolled into the subtle slide of her skin on mine.

She shifts up on her toes to worship my mouth. My hands slide down to hold her waist, lightly, chastely, while she paints possibilities with her tongue.

It's sweet. It's hot. The soft moan that escapes her turns me on like crazy. I want to bury my face in her neck, inhale her floral scent, lose myself in all she is.

It's so fucking good, but it hurts, too. She's inside me, everywhere, and half of me wants to push her out while the other half wants to open up, to let her in.

The second she threads her fingers in my hair, tugging greedily for more access, my control snaps.

She can't promise me all of her forever, but I'll take all of her tonight.

I press her up against the door, and with everything in me, I kiss her back.

Under the dress, she's slow curves that yield under the growing evidence of how much I want her. Annie's lips part, her breath coming in short gasps.

I reach for the keys in her hand and take them from her, fumbling to get the door open. We trip inside, her heels clicking on the wood floor. I turn her, press her back against the wall as the door closes behind us.

Before we broke up, I felt powerless. In the moments we'd lost ourselves in physicality, trying to connect in any way we could, we somehow missed each other.

This is the opposite.

I kiss her in the kitchen while she kicks off her shoes, in the living room as I unbutton my shirt. I kiss her in her bedroom, ignoring the desire to look around. Curiosity can wait. We've waited long enough.

I unzip her dress, slide the straps off her smooth shoulders, and watch it fall to the floor.

The way she looks at me, hungry eyes filled with lust and emotion, makes me want to hurry.

I don't.

I've never had a problem with patience, but I've had a problem with appreciation.

I won't take a moment of this, of *her*, for granted again.

I strip away the rest of our clothes, piece by piece.

My shirt and pants.

Her bra and panties.

I'm covered in ink, the words I could never say painting pictures across my body like she used to do with her pen.

She's slim and unmarked, a blank canvas that's familiar and fresh at once.

I touch every inch of her, cupping her breasts that fit perfectly in my hands, sucking her dark nipples until she moans my name.

My lips caress her shoulders, her throat, her waist, her hips.

I make love to her the way I've wanted to for weeks, years.

For the first time, I'm not afraid of what's between us. I take it all.

I touch her body as if she's mine forever instead of just for now.

She kisses me with the openness she's always had, the confidence that's new.

Her palm slips between us to wrap around me, forcing a hiss from my throat as pleasure spirals up my spine. Every muscle in me clenches, right down to the hand I spent two years hating...

And I want more.

I want her around me, so tight I can't breathe.

Inside me, in the space between the atoms that make up my muscles and skin and bones.

When the fire inside me won't be checked, I walk her toward the dresser, lifting her. She studies me with half-lidded eyes under dark lashes as our lips brush.

"Are you..."

My words are hoarse, the first sound in the silence that's not the slide of fabric or the pant of breath or the moan of a sigh.

Annie nods. "Do it," she whispers.

Four words.

They're all we need tonight.

When I press inside her, it's slow. I thank a god I've never prayed to before as every inch of her takes every inch of me.

I memorize the way her eyes change color when she's full of me. I devour her sighs and moans.

This is home.

This is love.

This is everything I've missed, everything I've wanted and never dared to name.

I'm lost with her, but for once, lost doesn't feel like panic. It feels like trust.

When she shudders in my arms, her mouth coming back to mine as if she can't stand to be apart from me, I know the truth.

I told myself I could make do with her giving me all of her tonight.

But it's not enough. It will never be enough.

14

Annie

Tyler Adams is a sore loser.

We play games on the plane back from New York. It's been a while since I traveled first class, but with him, I wouldn't care if we were stuffed in with the bags. Sitting next to him, hearing him laugh and seeing him smile, is amazing and maddening.

"It's a word game app," he argues, jerking his chin at my phone in his hand for emphasis. "You're going to win by default."

"That's not true," I say, wrenching the device away from him. "Man up and compete already."

He narrows his gaze. "You're going to attack my masculinity in the middle of a commercial flight?"

Then I feel a tickling at my waist and stifle a surprised shriek. "Sorry," I say to the flight attendant and the cabin in general as I shove his hands away and face the front of the plane, flushing.

To him, I murmur, "You are a menace to society."

His curved lips brush my ear. "That's not what you called me last night."

My thighs squeeze together at his lowered voice because I think I'm wet again. We had sex three times before falling asleep, and twice more this morning.

How either of us is still horny defies logic and biology.

"You promised not to do that on the plane."

"Do what? Distract you with thoughts of what else we could be doing right now? Forgive me if two years is a long time and I'd rather be so deep inside you—"

I clap a hand over his mouth because if he finishes that sentence, I'm going to come right in the middle of first class.

I shove my phone in my bag because there's no way I can concentrate on a game now.

After the flight attendant comes around to offer us drinks—we both opt for water, which comes in individual bottles with fancy glasses on the side—he asks, "So how does Mr. Douchey Ex not being involved affect your show?"

"If Ian's not the first investor, I need to line up

some alternatives. And the truth is he was our best chance because he knew us and knew our work."

I pull out my tablet and open up the files I started to pull while we waited for our flight.

"Bios," I explain as he looks over my shoulder. "On every other funder in Ian's circle of friends."

"Blackmail?"

I laugh. "Not quite. I know what they've invested in, what their history is. Ian's not going to do me any favors, but I'm hoping he won't interfere. Still, on the chance he won't...I need a Plan B."

His slow grin has me arching a brow.

"You're sexy when you're plotting," he decides.

I laugh, realizing we haven't talked much about serious stuff in the past week. "Thank you. What about you? Why are you chasing women to New York instead of working on new music?"

Tyler leans in. "I told you, I'm on a break. I'm getting surgery."

"But you've already had surgery."

"This'll be the fourth time."

My heart squeezes as the pieces click into place.

He's still trying to fix it. He might be past holding a grudge against the world and more relaxed with himself, but he doesn't believe he's as good as he was.

"Listen to what Zeke sent me." He digs out his phone, and I pop in the wireless headphones he offers.

The track streams out, and I listen. "How much did you contribute to this?" I ask after the first chorus, pulling out the headphones.

"I didn't."

"There's your problem."

Tyler looks past me, idly scanning the first-class cabin as if he's reaching for patience. "I'm not going to write something if I can't play it."

"Why not? Music is in your head and your heart, not your fingers. Especially when you live and breathe it. You could lose every sense you have and still feel it."

I pop the headphones back in and listen to the chorus once more, making some notes on the cocktail napkin in front of me.

"I don't know why you're trying to take a studio song and make it work for me. I can't make the music I want." He rubs a hand over his jaw. The morning scruff is giving me all kinds of ideas of where I'd like to feel it.

"Maybe you can make something better. You know," I go on when he doesn't respond, "It's cute how much you care about putting Shay in the studio."

He picks at his armrest. "I don't."

"But you do. You barely know her, but you want her to succeed, because she's talented."

The Tyler I knew before wouldn't have been as

invested in someone else. It gives me hope.

Not only for Shay, but also for him.

"What about you and your dad?" he comes back. "You still look stiff when you're in the same room together."

"I told you I found out Dad paid my tuition through an anonymous scholarship. Which means he didn't think I could do it on my own."

"Or he didn't want to watch you struggle. He loves you, Annie. Maybe he doesn't express it right, or use the words you want, but he does love you."

"What does that mean—like how you're all action and I'm all talk?" I tease.

"That's part of it. But I meant more like the way you can imagine your mom loved you, even though you've never met her."

The words land between us, and I blink to make sure I heard him right.

"That's not true."

Tyler's eyes soften but he doesn't press.

"If it was a big deal," I go on, "don't you think I would've contacted her? I don't need to. I didn't even know about her until I got that letter four years ago."

"Yeah, but the difference is now, even if you don't mean to, even if he doesn't know it, you're comparing him to her."

I fold my arms over my chest, staring at the water

glass, the liquid vibrating slightly with the movement of the plane.

"So what? You think if I want to square things with my dad, I have to contact her?"

Tyler's hand covers mine, and he tugs it toward him, threading our fingers together. Warmth spreads through me. "You don't have to do anything. But I don't want to see it eat at you."

I shift in my seat. "Did you make peace with your dad and what he did to you? The bills he left you with after?"

Tyler's head drops back against the headrest, but his eyes stay on me. "Yeah, I did. It took a long fucking time, but I did."

I turn that over the rest of the ride back to Dallas.

When the plane arrives, the car drops Tyler off at his hotel, then takes me back to Dad and Haley's. I walk in the door and immediately know something's wrong.

"Sophie, we need to go." My dad's voice is harsh as he stalks into the hallway.

"I don't wannoo. I'm playing."

My attention goes to Haley, who's hunched over by the stairs.

"What happened?" I demand, rushing to her.

"I've been having some headaches, which isn't a big deal except I don't normally get them," Haley says weakly. "Today I've been having stomach pains, too. I'm sure it's fine."

"I'm not," my dad responds. "We're going to the hospital now."

My dad and Haley take one car, and I drive Sophie in the other, following them. At the hospital, they take Haley and my dad into a room. Sophie and I wait outside.

I debate only the briefest moment before calling Tyler to tell him what happened.

"I'll be right there," he says immediately, and some of the worry ebbs away knowing he's coming.

I try to keep Sophie occupied, but she races to the door that opens to where Haley is. I'm a beat late chasing her.

Inside, the doctor's trying to kick out my dad. "We need to run some tests. It will be more efficient with only me here."

"Fuck efficient."

"Jax, it's fine," Haley insists, wrapping a hand around his wrist, which seems to soothe him. He seems more worked up than she does. "Go sit outside. How would you feel if someone was in your studio telling you what to do?"

Dad finally relents.

The three of us walk into the waiting room just as Tyler stalks around the corner.

"How is she?" Tyler asks, his gaze flicking between us.

"We're trying to find out," Jax answers grimly.

"Hey, Sunshine Sophie." Tyler's attention lands on my sister wandering down the hallway and tracing a finger down the wall. "Let's go find some trucks outside."

She runs for him, and I shoot him a grateful smile.

After Tyler departs, my dad lifts his hands to his face, and I frown. "Are you biting your nails right now?"

He rubs a hand over his neck. "Haven't done that in a long fucking time."

Beneath the grumpiness, there's something deeper, a worry that barking at people can't fix.

I think of my conversation with Tyler on the plane about loving people, and how we show our love in different ways. Dad definitely has the protective kind down.

"Come on," I say. "Let's go find snacks."

We head for the vending machines.

"Remember when we used to get BBQ Pringles for road trips?" I say, pulling out a bill and feeding it into the machine. "I haven't had them in years."

I punch the button and watch the silver spiral

thingy turn. It stops with the chips hanging from the edge. "Crap."

My dad shakes the machine, and I laugh as I feed it another bill.

He grunts. "It'll eat your money twice."

"It might not."

We both watch as if this is the most important thing in the world. The gear turns, dropping the first chips.

The second...

Nope. Stuck.

I drop into a chair, and he takes the one next to me.

I grab the tin and open the lid. "You do the honors."

He pops it and takes the first chip. "How was New York?"

The question is forced out, as if it takes an unusual amount of energy for him to expel the words.

"I had a minor setback with work," I say carefully, knowing my career hasn't been something we could talk about in the past. "A personal contact was going to invest in the new show. It got messy, and he's not the right fit anymore."

"It's a big deal, producing a show."

"I know."

I reach for a chip and crunch into it. He sits in silence next to me.

"Tyler kicked my kid out of the studio and wants to put Shay in his place," he goes on after a moment. "I didn't bring him on to scout talent. I brought him on to rein it in. He was always sensible at that age. Mostly sensible," he amends. "I put a lot into this label. My reputation. My money."

I cock my head. "If you lose everything, Haley has her business. She can support you."

He shoots me side-eye, and I can't help smiling.

"Everyone thinks dating musicians is awesome," I say. "But it sucks."

My dad follows my gaze down the hall to where Tyler's playing with Sophie.

"Am I the reason you're not with Tyler?"

The words are so quiet I almost miss them.

"No. We're...I don't know what we are," I admit. "But after he got hurt, we needed space. I told myself he needed something I couldn't give him. But I wanted my dreams too. I wanted to prove I could make it."

"And now?"

I exhale hard. "I don't know, Dad."

"He cares about you." He looks over at me. "Haley will be the first to say I'm not patient. Loving someone doesn't mean you're a different person every day. But it means you're willing to try to be better."

I offer him the last chip.

He shakes me off. "It's yours."

I break it in half, and he takes the other part.

"You know which album is the most important?" he muses after finishing and brushing his hands on his jeans. "It's the one you create next. It's not just about the money. It's my reputation."

"That's why you should trust Tyler about Shay." I glance toward the man I love entertaining my little sister down the hall, and my chest expands until it threatens to crack my ribs. "Because he doesn't go all in every day. But when he does... it's magic."

15

Tyler

"That thing you wanted me to keep an eye out for? I've got a lead on it," Beck says over the phone as I shift out of my car at the studio the next day. "Four bedrooms. Ocean view. Floor-to-ceiling glass. Don't drool on your shoes."

I shake my head as I grab the front door and head inside. Shay waves at me, and I nod. "Get the realtor to chase it down for me."

"Done. Long as I get first dibs on bedrooms."

I've been saving for a place on the beach. My plan is to get my surgery, fix my hand, and get back to my album in warm weather—no more cold winters that make my hand feel useless and broken.

But that's not the only reason for my upbeat mood.

I could chalk it up to my surgery coming up soon, but it's not that.

It's the time I'm spending with Annie, but also creatively, helping Shay.

Hell, I even started work with the songs Zeke sent me, though I'm not about to admit it until I go back to LA.

Which I have to do soon.

But it's been easy to push that from my mind in light of the chaos of the past few days.

I hang up and glance at Shay, who's unpacking her things at her desk.

"Ready to work?" I ask her.

"Absolutely." Her face lights up with enthusiasm. "First, though, you have guests waiting in your office." I frown, and she hurries to add, "They said they knew you."

I start back there, annoyed someone's in there without me. I push the door wide and stop in my tracks.

Annie's inside, looking like everything right in the world in a flowy blue dress that makes me want to press her up against the wall and find out if she's wearing anything under it.

"Hey, beautiful. How's Haley this morning?"

"Resting but good. No more pains. And the headaches have subsided."

Last night we got back from the hospital around

midnight, after the doctors ran a bunch of tests and diagnosed Haley with preeclampsia. Given she's not due to deliver for another month, they gave her medication and advised her to stick to bed rest and return if things worsened.

I go to kiss Annie, but she pulls back. "Slow your roll, Romeo. We've got company."

She moves out of the way to reveal Rae slouched in my task chair.

I arch a brow at Annie's former roommate. "You look comfortable."

"Lumbar support is important," Rae deadpans. But she rises from her chair and I grab her in a one-armed hug she reluctantly allows.

Annie says, "She's stopped over on her way to Miami for a DJ gig."

"Damn. I was just talking to Beck. He'll be bummed he missed you."

"What were you talking about?" Annie asks, and my chest tightens as I think about the house.

"Ah... nothing. You wanna see Jax's new artist?"

I lead them to the studio where Shay's getting set. I nod at her to start.

Through the glass, Rae watches intently. She and Annie are both looking for different things than I would—I can tell from the way they watch, the way they listen. It's the beautiful thing about music—everyone gets something different from it.

Rae folds her arms over her chest. "She any good in front of a crowd?"

"She's playing tonight," I say. "You should come. Both of you."

When Annie and her friend take off, I hold her back for a moment in the hallway to kiss her until she melts under my hands.

"Mmm," she murmurs when I pull back. "What was that for?"

"Your dad texted to give me the green light on Shay. Funny how that happened when he was completely opposed to it yesterday."

Her eyes sparkle. "So weird."

It means she and her dad are talking, and Jax is holding up his end of our bargain.

I kiss her again, hard, before letting her go. "Thanks."

Annie tosses me a look over her shoulder as she heads for the door. "Any time."

Since New York, things between us have felt good.

We haven't had a "where is this headed" conversation, which doesn't feel right given we're finally spending time together again.

But even though I don't know the specific answer, I know I don't want to lose her.

After I finish working with Shay, I open my email to find a brutal reality check.

The note from Zeke's office is brief but outlines expectations of my contract once I'm back in LA—which I'm supposed to be in another week. There are a dozen attachments. I only open the first two—a schedule for studio time, tens of thousands of dollars' worth, plus an invitation to a party.

The last few weeks, I have been checked out. I needed the time.

I need more time.

My gut twists.

The email is a reminder this is all temporary, that I'm heading back to LA soon—not just for my surgery, but for my life.

I'm heading across the parking lot when Annie's voice from across the fence stops me. "Where are you going?"

"Home for a shower and to change before Shay's show." I cross to where she's standing, slide a hand between the fence posts, and wrap my arm around her waist.

Her lips curve. "I got some good writing done today."

"Sing for me?"

Annie laughs. "You listened to musicians all day long."

"None I wanted to fuck."

Her gaze drops down my body. "You have a

change of clothes in the office? You could have dinner with us at the house. Shower after."

Twenty minutes later, we're arranged around the table in Jax's dining room. Sophie's devouring chicken fingers while the rest of us have grilled salmon.

"Forgive the catering," Haley says. "It's been a busy few weeks, and it's getting busier before it gets easier."

"This is great. Thanks, Haley," I say, and she smiles. "Shay's set is tonight," I remind Jax. "You could come."

He turns it over, glancing at Annie. "It's fine. My wife could pop any minute."

Haley rolls her eyes. "Jax, I'm not going to pop."

They share a smile that makes me cut a look at Annie.

"How's work going?" Haley asks Annie.

"I'm so close to finishing the last song. The reading is scheduled for the first week of September. It's a chance for a number of people to show off new ideas. Ian's assistant organizes it and he hosts, but there are lots of other contacts there."

"Ian's the ex," Jax says gruffly.

"He's one of those guys who wears suits for fun," I add before Annie can speak.

Jax's gaze narrows. "A douche."

"First-class."

Annie's jaw drops, and Haley hides a smile behind her napkin.

"Thank you for those uninvited opinions on my love life. You don't know anything about him," Annie tosses.

My muscles tighten in response, my voice lowering. "I know he had you and he let you go."

Silence falls over the table as I hold her stare.

I remember what Jax asked me once: whether I loved Annie the way he loved Haley.

I do. I know it, which only makes the reality of our situation harder.

"Anyway," Annie goes on at last, a flush crawling up her cheeks that makes me want to drag her to the nearest room or closet or front-fucking-lawn and devour her. "These funders like to go in on things together. But, I've learned that a few of Ian's friends have invested independently in the last ten years. So I'm going to focus on them."

After dinner, Annie crooks a finger at me and I follow her down the hall.

"Where are you going?" Jax asks.

Annie tosses him a look. "Tyler and I are going to hang out, Dad," she says in a mock-whiny-teenager voice.

He grumbles something inaudible before heading back toward the kitchen, and I laugh under my breath.

"He wants to make sure we're not having sex in the shower," I tell her as we ascend the stairs.

At the top, she turns, peering up at me. "You don't want to have sex in the shower?"

Her innocent voice sends every ounce of blood to my dick.

"Fucking yes, I do."

She laughs as we get to her room and shut the door behind us.

As I strip off her clothes and make her mine, one slow drugging kiss at a time, I wish I could shut the door on LA and my fears just as easily.

After dinner, we meet Rae at the venue where Shay's playing.

Thanks to a delicious dinner and the fact that I made Annie come twice in the shower and once more in her bed, tonight's already feeling like a solid win. Now, I try to push the email from Zeke from my mind as I get ready to share the night with the woman I love and her friend, watching an artist that I found and nurtured.

As we crowd around a high top table, Annie pries stories from Rae her life on the road as a DJ trying to make it. The woman's always been hard to get a read on, but I'm fascinated hearing her experiences.

Unlike me, she sounds like she could travel forever.

"You okay?" Annie asks, leaning over.

I slide a hand over her knee, resting my fingers on the inside of her thigh as I brush my lips across her jaw. "Yeah."

I look up as the band starts, and Shay takes the mic, but she's not looking at the crowd—she's looking at the floor.

Alarm stirs low in my gut. I can't put my finger on the warning feeling, but I know something's off.

"What is she doing?" Rae asks.

She misses her cue, and the band keeps playing. Eventually, they stop. Annie and I exchange a look, but we both know.

Shay's frozen up.

I'm cursing her for it even as I weave through the crowd to the foot of the stage. I shoot security a look as they spring into action, but they stop when they recognize me.

Shay's eyes widen as she sees me leap onto the stage. "I'm sorry," she whispers hoarsely when I stop in front of her.

"It's fine. You got this," I say.

"I know. I thought I did, but... Just don't go anywhere, okay?"

I nod to the confused band, and they restart.

I step back into the wings and nod at her.

Her gaze is locked on mine as she sings the first line. It's tentative.

The guitarist is eyeing us warily, so I grab his unused mic and join in.

Shay's smile lights up the entire place.

I keep going, and she finds her stride.

By the time we hit the chorus together, the audience is loving it.

It feels good to be up there, better still to help her.

My hand might be fucked but the way Shay's looking at me from the stage and Annie's looking at me from the audience, it's hard to believe anything is missing in this moment.

After, I head back down the stairs, surprised to see Annie and even Rae holler and applaud as I rejoin them.

"Well, that was a disaster."

"It was averted, and you made something even better together," Annie corrects.

I search her gaze, my chest expanding. "You're good for my soul," I say simply.

She grabs my arms, her hands digging into my biceps. "I know you don't like thinking of yourself as depending on other people or having them depend on you..." she goes on, "But you matter. To your friends. To me. To Shay. You can make a difference here. With my dad and in people like Shay's lives."

My chest tightens. Not her life.

I tuck her hair behind her ear. "When I was on tour, I realized I couldn't blame what happened to me for how I felt. But I also promised myself I'd do whatever it took to be as good as I was before. And while I was at it," I go on, my mouth tugging up at the corner, "I'd get a house on the beach. Somewhere warm. Somewhere I'd wake up every day and make music I love and not owe anyone anything.

"It's the security I've always wanted, Annie. The freedom. And you helped me get it."

She stiffens, love and sadness competing on her face. "I'm glad."

"Before I left for tour, I told you I wished you'd never made me dream. That's not true, and I never should have said it."

"Tyler...it's okay."

"It's not. Because I need you to know that I still dream. And when I dream, I dream of us.

"You telling me about your work on the couch while we watch the sun set after a long day. Me getting you roses because you love them even when you have no earthly reason to. You swimming naked in our pool until I'm so turned on I have to take you right there."

Her eyes darken, and I wish we weren't in public so I could show her how fucking good it could be.

"Is that all?" she murmurs at last, looking understandably overwhelmed.

No.

I want kids who glare at us with your eyes and scream at us with my mouth.

I want you and me forever.

I want you to want it as badly as I do.

But I can't ask because there's a huge hole in my chest even with her standing right in front of me, one that'll get bigger the moment she says that's not what she wants.

"Yeah," I say instead. "That's all."

16

Annie

There's nothing like the morning after a night that doesn't end.

Last night I rewrote the final song for the musical completely while staring at the studio before falling asleep in my chaise lounge, my notebook on my lap.

The fog I've been wrestling with cleared and I accomplished what I've been trying to for months.

I was so sure of it, I took a screenshot and sent it off to Miranda last night.

When the sun comes up, a slice of vibrant orange on the horizon, the paper is on the patio next to my chair. My phone buzzes with a message from my writing partner.

It's short and sweet.

. . .

Miranda: That's it.

Satisfaction and pride settle in me as I shift out of the chair, rubbing a hand through my hair.

The tile cool under my bare feet, I stretch my sore muscles, thinking of the routine I've established since I returned from New York.

Helping with Sophie in the morning, taking her to school.

Hanging with Haley when my dad's working, half to keep an eye on her and half because she's fun and super smart and the kind of woman I want to be.

Dropping in on Tyler around lunch—midafternoon if I can wait that long—to hang out, which often ends with us sweaty and naked.

But yesterday he played me Shay's track, which is sounding freaking awesome, plus a couple of new bands he's thinking about sending to my dad. I teased him about being a wannabe A&R guy.

"When I dream, I dream of us."

When he said the words, I wanted to wrap my arms around him and never let him go.

Because I love spending time with him. I love how he is with Shay, how she's slowly dragging him out of his own head where his music is concerned.

He's so different than he was when we broke up, and better still for having spent these weeks here.

And so am I.

I'm more comfortable with myself. I don't have every answer, and I'm okay with that. I'm not afraid someone will accuse me of not being capable enough to write a musical, or star in a show, or be unreasonable because I want to be in the spotlight and be part of a family.

Dad and I can have a conversation one-on-one, not just be civil for a meal, I like helping Haley and Sophie, and most of all I love that the only guy who's ever owned my heart is right here.

I considered walking away from my dreams to run after Tyler two years ago, and it would've been a mistake. He needed the space to figure out a new normal, and I needed to prove to myself I could hack it in the city.

So what if this time is different?

I head upstairs and take a shower, luxuriating in the hot steam for a few minutes before I pull on jean shorts and a tank top and head to Sophie's room. I crack the pink curtains before dropping to my knees next to the bed.

I tickle her face. "Good morning. Time for daycare, Soph."

She wrinkles her nose and swats my hand. "It's not."

Her sleepy mumble has me laughing.

"It is."

"Sing me a song." I start to, and her eyes blink open. "I don't know that one."

I brush the hair back from her face. "No one does yet. I wrote it."

"Sing more."

"When you get up."

She's out of bed in a second. If my audiences are as receptive as Sophie, maybe this new show has a shot.

She picks out her clothes, and I pull her hair back and braid it, the only part she'll let me do.

When we get downstairs, there's a figure looming at the sliding doors.

"*Tyler!*" Sophie runs over, pressing up on her toes to stubbornly work the lock until she can let him in.

"Thanks, Sunshine Sophie." His hands are full of a huge basket with fancy decaf and other treats, which he lifts. "For Haley."

"What about for me?" Sophie prompts.

I'm about to tell her we're making her cereal, but Tyler frowns and rummages in the basket, pulling out a purple plastic truck. "I don't see anything for you."

She jumps on the toy.

"I got it in LA, but it's been living in my hotel room ever since," he murmurs to me.

My stomach twists, every part of me tingling.

"I love you," I blurt.

Tyler's smile freezes. He squares to face me, his handsome face surprised and pleased. "I love you too."

The words sink into my skin, my bones, my soul.

I want to hear him say it again.

"I love you both," Sophie says solemnly, and I can't help laughing as Tyler ruffles her hair.

"All right, time for cereal," I say, heading for the cupboards.

Sophie runs toward the front door before I can argue, comes back a moment later with shoes, and drops them at Tyler's feet. "Shoes first."

Apparently, she's decided she wants him at her beck and call.

Can't say I blame her.

"Shoes at the same time," Tyler counters.

She hops into her chair and puts on her bib.

"Sing your song for Tyler," she commands as she starts to munch.

I sing, pouring a black coffee for me and one with cream for Tyler. When I turn back to him, mug in hand, he's watching with fascination.

"That's it," Tyler murmurs when I finish.

"Funny. Miranda said the same thing."

As Tyler and I drink our coffees and Sophie finishes her cereal, my dad comes down the steps and takes in the scene.

"Daddy!" She scoots out of her chair and into his arms. "Annie wrote a song. It's the best song."

"Annie writes all the best songs," Dad responds.

"How would you know?" I toss.

"My favorite is this one."

He starts to sing one from my other musical and Sophie squeals in delight. "Let's get you to school, kid," he tells Sophie once he finishes.

I'm still struggling with the emotion that comes from realizing he knows one of my songs.

It never occurred to me that he did.

But as my gaze finds Tyler's, I know he can see it all on my face.

"How's Haley?" I ask Dad as Sophie finishes her breakfast and goes to grab her backpack.

"Tired but in good spirits. I shouldn't be going to this party in LA."

I cross to him and squeeze his arm. "It'll be okay. Serena's coming tomorrow to stay, so she, Haley, Sophie, and I can do a girls' night. Besides, everyone's going to this party, right?"

"Yeah." He nods in response, giving me a one-armed hug.

"So, maybe Shay should go."

Dad looks between me and Tyler as I hold my breath.

"Yes," Dad decides. "Shay should go."

Tyler shoves both hands in his pockets. "I'll let her know."

They leave, and I jump on Tyler. "I'm so glad Shay's working out."

"Thanks to you."

"No, thanks to you," I point out. "You're the one who pushed for her. I just helped move things along."

I plant a kiss on him, then take the treats he brought up to Haley, who thanks me.

"No treats for you?" I ask Tyler when I'm back downstairs.

He looks up from his phone before tucking it away. "I have very discriminating standards."

"Bullshit." I grab a bowl and the box of Rice Krispies. "You'd fuck someone for Circle Krispies."

He groans as he crosses to me. "If that someone is you?" he murmurs against my neck, wrapping an arm around me to drag my hips against his, "I'd fuck you for dryer lint."

I laugh, but every part of me lights up. I reluctantly pull back and pass him the bowl of butter and marshmallows. "We should probably make some Circle Krispies for Sophie."

"The kid's going to be a walking marshmallow."

"Didn't hurt us."

He chuckles and melts the marshmallows.

"Why don't we get sick of these after so many

years?" I ask. "I can't decide if it's the sweetness or the chewiness."

"It's because we always made them together."

God, my aching heart.

I cast a look over my shoulder, thinking about the email sitting in my inbox since yesterday, the one I've read a dozen times. "I emailed my mom. She's in LA. She said she'd meet me."

Tyler closes the distance between us. "Wow. That's huge. You could come to LA with us when we go for the party. You don't even have to tell your dad the reason."

I turn that over. "Maybe I will. What kind of activity says, 'We've never met, but let's connect as grownups'?"

"Fly fishing."

I laugh. "Or drinks. Somewhere quiet but not so quiet you can feel the awkwardness."

"I can suggest a few places."

"Thanks." We share a smile.

"You're so good with Sophie," I can't help saying. "You want kids?"

"Depends who with. I figured you and I'd have three. The first one to practice. The second would be the refined model. The third, just because we were so fucking good at making the first two."

I nearly drop the wooden spoon.

The microwave beeps, and he removes the bowl

before turning back to me. "We didn't have great childhoods, but we wouldn't put our kids through that. It doesn't mean everything would go smoothly, but we'd love the hell of out of them."

Tyler sets the bowl on the counter and takes the spoon from between my fingers, as if he didn't blow me apart a second ago with this wild and enthralling idea of us procreating.

We're too young to think about it, but I know Tyler would be a great dad. He'd be caring and patient and consistent. He'd always take an interest, have a sense of humor about things too.

"Are you asking me to have your kids?" I try to make it a joke, to hide the longing in my voice.

He traces the handle down my forehead, my nose, my lips. "I'm telling you I've thought about it. With you, I've thought about everything."

My heart squeezes and I try to make sense of the jumble of feelings and thoughts swirling inside me.

"So you'll come to LA when we go?" he asks abruptly before I can respond.

"I don't see why not. But aside from hitching a ride on the charter, what's the rush?"

He heaves out a breath. "Because after this party...I'm staying in LA. My hand surgery is next week and after that, I'm scheduled to go back into the studio."

"Oh." The backs of my eyes burn.

He threads the fingers of his good hand into my hair, pulling me against him.

I want to tell him not to go, but that feels petty and childish. I know it's not only the logistics that are keeping us apart. The last time I went all in on him, I lost him. We're older now, smarter, but the possibility of him changing his mind, or of the lives we're building coming between us, is the most awful thing I can imagine.

He moves behind me, wraps his arms around my waist. "Sing me that song again."

I close my eyes and give in to the feeling and do as he asks.

I pretend for a moment it could always be this way—him asking for things, me knowing I can give them to him, that I can make this man happy. This man who, by breathing, gives me so damned much.

"It's beautiful," he says. "What happens when this pitch session goes well?"

Needing to distance myself even a few inches, I mix the cereal into the bowl, then spread the mixture into a pan, pressing it down with a wooden spoon.

"*If* it goes well," I amend, "we get commitment to move forward." I take the pan to the freezer and return to him. "Then, if we keep meeting stage gates and the reception is strong... we could be off-Broadway in one year. On Broadway in two or three."

"Years. In New York."

Hope swells inside me, but it's bittersweet. "That's the dream. And it is a dream, Tyler. For so long I've wanted to be in the spotlight. I thought it was about me, but after doing the first show, I learned it's more than that. When you're performing live, you get to be intimate with people. Whether it's a few hundred or thousands, they're not a crowd. You're touching every person in that audience. People like us who are questioning if they've got it figured out, or who know they don't and can't see a way forward. People who need a flash of inspiration, something out of the ordinary. People who need to feel something real."

He watches me steadily as he strokes a thumb down my cheek. "I have a call with my label this afternoon, but if you want someone to rehearse with first…"

"I'd love that."

Tyler's eyes crinkle at the corners. "Then let's go to work. I'm all yours."

But my chest aches because I want the second part of his vow more than the first.

17

Annie

"Table for Annie Jamieson," I tell the woman at the front of the trendy restaurant in LA.

I follow her back to a table tucked into the corner.

"You requested something with privacy. How's this?" she asks.

"Perfect. Thank you." I sit facing the door and watch people drift in.

The full weight of my attention is on this meeting.

I don't even know this woman, but I want to like her—and I want her to like me.

I smooth the skirt of my simple black dress and wonder if I should've worn my hair up instead of down.

The nerves didn't hit me when I confirmed the meeting time, not even on the charter flight with my dad, Tyler, and Shay earlier today.

They're hitting me now.

A waitress comes by and offers me the drink menu. "Would you like something?"

"Sure, I'll have a glass of pinot grigio."

I recognize her the second she walks in. Her hair is red like mine, and her mouth pulls into a startled smile.

"Annie. Oh my God."

I shift out of my seat as her gaze runs over me. "You're beautiful."

Her eyes mist, and I let her hug me.

"Hi... Fiona." I can't say "Mom." The word sticks in my throat. "Thank you for meeting me."

She's beautiful too, early forties and still completely fresh-faced and slender, her black jump-suit revealing long, tanned legs.

"I was surprised to hear from you after all this time."

"I'm sorry it took so long. I wasn't ready."

Her brows pull together. "Of course."

The waitress comes by to offer wine, and Fiona jumps at it.

"Tell me everything," she says once the waitress departs to get our drinks.

"I'm not sure where to start," I confess with a smile.

"Wherever you want."

So I tell her about how I grew up in Dallas, then attended Vanier for two years before getting a gig working with Miranda Talbot writing a new show for the stage.

"You're writing for Broadway," she gushes as two glasses are set in front of us. "I always wanted to be on Broadway. Do you think you'd have a role for me?"

I shift in my seat. "We haven't even gotten funding, not to mention cast it. But maybe? It will be a lot of work until previews."

"Oh, I see." Her face falls. "You must know everyone in the business."

I start to say "no," but I stop at the last minute. "I have worked with a lot of people. I've kept pretty busy since school. And every person I meet teaches me something."

"I'm sure. There are so many rich, handsome men in New York," she insists.

"Right." It takes effort to hold my smile in place. "But tell me about you. How long have you been in LA?"

"Ages. I've done commercials. And guest appearances on a couple of network shows," she says with pride. "But I've always known there's something bigger out there for me. Do you feel that way?"

My chest expands at her description. I know that feeling. I've lived it.

Maybe it didn't come from the world.

Maybe it came from the woman in front of me.

"Yes. I do."

Her eyes glint as she reaches over the table and covers my hand with hers. "How's Jax? I heard he launched a label recently."

"He's excited. He's actually in LA, too, for an event later tonight."

The second the words are out, Fiona sucks in a breath. "And you're going? I'd love to see him again. And meet some of your friends."

The way she says it has me hesitating. "From the letter you wrote to me, I figured you and my dad hadn't parted ways on the best of terms."

"Well, I'm sure we've all moved past it now. He's quite a charmer. We'd have plenty to laugh about now. Is his wife at this party too?"

I slide my hand out from under hers to reach for my wine even though my stomach is suddenly unsettled.

"She's not. And as for the party—I don't know the host well enough to invite a friend. Dad's focused on promoting a new artist."

She seems to sense me shutting down and leans

in. "Well, I bet the money is better in music than the stage."

"Probably," I concede. "I don't think people go to Broadway for the money. But if you want to be part of something incredible and touch people every night, it's the place to be."

Fiona laughs. "It sounds exhausting."

I try to keep the conversation on her because every time it comes back to me, I end up feeling as if she cares more about what I can do for her than who I am, what I like.

We finish our glasses of wine, and I make my excuses before putting her in a cab to go home with a hug that's shorter on my end than hers, one I wish I could lean into but can't.

By the time the car pulls away, I'm actually aching to go to an industry party with the people I love.

"How did I score two handsome dates to this event?" I ask.

"Correction. *I* scored two handsome dates." Beck shifts across the back seat in the limo and hooks an arm around my neck.

Five of us are in the limo—Dad, Shay, Beck, Tyler, and me. High-end carpooling isn't usually feasible in LA, but Beck surprised us by showing at our hotel, so he came with us.

Despite the weird meeting with my mom and the fact that tomorrow, I'll be on a plane leaving this city without Tyler, I'm grateful for the company tonight.

My dad looks up from his phone for the first time and shakes his head.

"Haley will be okay," I insist. "Serena's with her."

"You won't miss your kid being born, Big J," Beck states.

We get out of the limo, Shay lingering behind.

I grab her arm and whisper in her ear, "You recorded a single this week that'll be the first release from my dad's new label. This is your coming-out party."

"I'm not sure I want one."

Her uncertainty has empathy rising up.

"He didn't either," I say, nodding toward Tyler, his confident strides eating up the sidewalk.

At the doors, Tyler turns, looking for me. "You ready?"

"You bet." I take his arm.

We make our way past security into the house of a huge producer. I've been to these parties in New York, though a Chelsea loft party has a different feel than a house in the Hills.

This is spacious, like our house but with a killer view. The house is modern, all glass, with doors swept wide open out to a marble terrace with an infinity pool. A five-piece band is playing on one side of the pool.

When my dad takes Shay to meet the head of the biggest music magazine on the planet, Tyler huffs out a breath next to me.

"She's not ready."

"She'll figure it out." He holds my stare, but Beck and I drag him toward the bar. Beck insists on champagne all around.

"I have news," he declares, looking handsome in a pale-blue dress shirt that sets off his dark hair and eyes. "My pilot got picked up. We have a ten-episode run. We start filming Monday."

"That's amazing!" I hug him.

"Yeah. I play a cop with psychic powers."

"Wasn't that Jennifer Love Hewitt?"

He shrugs and settles his hands on my temples while Tyler looks entertained. "I see you going home with me tonight, gorgeous."

"Stick to acting." Tyler grabs Beck's arms and shoves them away.

Beck's eyes dance, and he looks past us. "Oh. No, I'm going home with him."

He takes off, and Tyler turns toward me, stepping close enough his jacket brushes my bare arm. "How are you? We haven't had a chance to talk alone since you met your mom."

I eye him in the twilight. "She was perfectly nice."

"But."

"But she wanted things other than me."

His expression clouds. "I'm sorry."

"I should've known. You were right. I thought she'd be good in all the ways he's not. Patient. Easy-going. Flexible. But it's easy to forget your parents' pluses."

Like that my dad cares about family way more than money.

The band plays Sinatra, and Tyler glances toward the half-full dance floor. He shifts so the railing is at his back, the soft lights playing over his handsome features.

"I want to ask you to dance. But if we do, everyone in here is going to know we're together. They'll be like, 'Who's that handsome asshole with Annie Jamieson?'"

I throw my head back and laugh. "No, they'll be like 'Who's that bitch with Tyler Adams?'"

He shakes his head. "He's probably in love with her," he continues in a mimicking voice.

I snort champagne up my nose, and the bubbles sting. "He's probably using her to get to Jax," I say in the same gossipy tone, searching out my dad and Shay on instinct.

"Except we know the truth."

I arch a brow, waiting.

"Her dad's not the prize. It's always been her."

My body tingles. He's watching me intently, intensely.

We're standing on the edge of the world, and it has nothing to do with the balcony or the view or the people.

My heart's telling me this moment is right—he's right. That in all the times I lost faith, I always came back to him. I love him. Not then. Now. Always. Tyler's the dream I never gave up on, and I never want to leave his side.

I thought my dream was this musical—it was the final way to cement my belonging in this industry in a way that felt right to me.

But I know I belong. Tyler helped me see that.

And listening to my heart, I know I have another dream.

Him. Us.

Maybe I could stay.

I take a slow breath, my heart pounding.

But before I can respond, my phone rings.

It's Miranda Talbot. "I have to take this."

I squeeze Tyler's arm, and he frowns but nods as I duck toward a quiet corner.

I answer her call. "Hi. What's up? It's after midnight where you are."

"Ian killed the reading."

Ice settles into my veins, and I blink back my

surprise. "Wait, what? It's been scheduled for months."

"He just sent a private email around to tell the other funders to say he's lost confidence in the direction of the show and won't host the reading."

Shock slams into me. "Shit. Can you reassure them?"

I have all their contact information from the research I've been doing.

"I can try, but my words will only go so far. I have other news. I didn't want to worry you until we knew for sure, but I've gotten a breast cancer diagnosis."

I nearly drop the phone as fear seizes my gut. "Miranda, are you okay?" My eyes squeeze shut. "Of course you're not okay. Tell me everything."

She explains how they found it, that they're looking at options. All I hear is that my writing partner and mentor's health is at risk.

We may not be the kind of friends who braid each other's hair, but since we began collaborating more than two years ago, I've learned so much from her. She's never let me down, and I'm not about to let her down.

And if we don't get this show, it would be letting her down. She's helped write others but this one is hers and mine. She never had children and this show is her baby.

"I'll come back," I promise, though my chest feels

as if it's caving in. "This weekend. I'll talk to the funders and find us a new host." The business side isn't my strength, but I'll make it work. "I promise I won't let you down."

When I go back to the party, I don't see Tyler. Panic is rising up in my chest, my throat.

I trip toward the exit, murmuring a quick "I'm fine" to the concerned security who asks if he can help on my way down the stairs.

At street level, I stagger outside and suck in air. The sounds of the music still drift down here, though aside from the soft lights of the house, it's mostly dark.

Talbot's news reverberates in the back of my mind.

I shove both hands in my hair and pace the road in front of the house, passing expensive cars parked along the way.

I have to finish the show—not for myself, but for Miranda, for the people who need it.

I have to...

I pull up as a shadowy figure emerges from the same door I left through a minute ago.

"Dad."

"I saw you come down and wanted to check on you." His voice is gruff, but there's an undercurrent of worry.

"Someone's trying to sink our show before it gets started."

He closes the distance between us, and I swallow, a million feelings colliding in my chest.

Disappointment. Worry. Despair.

"Tell me how I can help."

My exhale is shaky because those six words are *everything*. It's not like my dad to be so open without an agenda or without inserting his opinion.

But he's asking.

"Do you want to dance?"

His hand finds my waist, and I fit my palm in his.

He asks me about options, and I tell him what contacts I have, the timing that was planned and how we could make it up. He suggests some paths I hadn't thought of and listens.

By the time we're done, the song has changed twice, but we're still moving.

"I always saw the dark side of this business," he says. "But you find ways to make it brighter, to make it better from the inside out. It's easy to want to be a part of that. Hell, I wouldn't have started this label if it wasn't for you. What you've done made me rethink the industry. I realized I have more to contribute, and I can make it better instead of living under what it is."

The gentleness in his tone, the compassion, makes the backs of my eyes burn. "You mean it?"

Dad nods. "Our children have a way of being better than we are in ways we couldn't have imagined. When you have kids, you'll see it too."

He glances down at our feet. "You're pretty good at this dancing."

My lips curve. "I had to take so many classes. I felt like I was drowning."

"You never looked like it on stage."

Surprise works through me. "When did you see me?"

"Any time I could. Opening night. At the holidays. On your birthday." My fingers dig into his shoulders, and I force them to relax.

"But you didn't say anything."

"I knew I'd fucked up, and I didn't know how to fix it. You went through so much as a kid, and I always wanted to keep you from hurting more, so I tried to protect you. To insulate you. Instead, I made it worse."

The words come out stilted, as if he's confessing something he's held in for too long. I study his face in the half light. This is hard for him, harder than taking Tyler's advice on his new artist. Maybe even harder than starting a label.

It means that much more because it's hard.

"You didn't make it worse, Dad. I wouldn't be who I am if you hadn't been who you were. I remember going to one of your shows when I was a kid. We had front-row seats, and I was the only person under the age of sixteen. I was buzzing from the second the lights went down, and when you came out on stage, the way you looked..." I sigh. "I wanted to be that. I wanted to be you. I used to think it was because everyone loved you. But now, I think it was because even before I found out you were my dad... some part of me knew."

In this moment, I forgive him for all of it, because I know he's fighting to do the right thing, just like I am.

Even if he doesn't get it all the time...none of us do.

But a relationship isn't forged in a moment, and it isn't demolished in one, either. There's always something to be saved, if you want to save it.

"I love you, Dad," I say softly. "And I know I'm lucky to have you in my life."

His eyes shine, and if Jax Jamieson starts crying right now, I'm going to lose it.

"I love you too, kid. You get yours," he says gruffly. "This time, I'll be in the front row."

18

Tyler

The morning after the party, I wake up to the sound of my phone buzzing. I shift out of bed, taking a second to admire Annie next to me, her red hair splayed over the hotel pillow.

Last night, we got back from the party late.

I know it's been a lot for her meeting her birth mom and the pressure of finishing her show. I'm so damned proud of her even as I admire her for doing what she needs to even when she's afraid.

It's one more thing I love about her.

I tug on boxer briefs and head out to the balcony to answer the call from my realtor.

"What's up?" I say by way of an answer.

"That property you wanted is a go. You ready to

make an offer? If you don't, it'll go on the market, and there's no way you'll get another shot at it."

I tug the sliding glass door behind me.

It's what I've wanted for ages, and this is my chance. "I'll call you back."

"Today. I'll try to hold them off, but you're going to lose this place."

When I head back inside, Annie's in the shower.

I set my phone on the nightstand, and the text that came through while I was talking to my realtor has my abs clenching.

"Hey," Annie says when she gets out of the shower. "You ready for breakfast?"

I take a second to memorize the way her hair hangs in wet waves around her shoulders, how the towel leaves miles of her legs exposed.

"Yeah. Your dad said the charter is leaving at four. He hadn't heard from you, so he wanted to make sure you got the message."

Her smile fades as she realizes the same thing I do.

Today's our last day together, and it just got shorter.

"Tell me what you want," she murmurs. "We can stay in bed all day. I'll call the front desk and book the room for another night if we have to. Or we could go to the beach. We could shoot pool. I don't care as long as I'm with you."

I can't breathe because this feels so right, spending the day with her without an agenda.

But it also feels wrong as hell to know it's the last time we'll do it this summer.

"I want to show you something," I tell her.

I drive her to the house in Santa Monica and park outside.

"This is it?" she whispers.

"Yeah. Did you want to go inside? I can call the realtor. Have him meet us here."

Her eyes fill with tears.

"Shit," I mutter, shifting across the console to wrap an arm around her. "This is not what I was going for."

"It's not that. Last night, I wanted... I dream of you too, Tyler." she swallows. "This show in New York, it's not only my dream. It's other people's. I need to see it through—not because I want to prove I can, but for them."

I heave out a breath. I've never been willing to have people rely on me like that, but I love her for it.

"I hate this," I confess. "Not this time with you. I hate that I can be a part-time brother or friend or son. I can move in and out of Jax's life or Sophie's or Beck's or even Shay's. I can stop by for a weekend or a vacation, and we can catch up, and it's like old times. And thanks to you, I want to. I know what it's like to have people in my life I care about and who care about me.

"But I can't be with you part-time. You need someone with you always. Someone who's all in. Someone to wake up with, to laugh with. Someone to hold you when you're freaking out."

Her soft face, full of love and sadness and hope, has my chest caving in. "Maybe not. I could be in New York, and we could go back and forth."

"You *deserve* that, Annie. I couldn't live with the thought of you having less than you deserve." She's too bright, too creative, too connected. "And this sounds selfish as fuck, but letting you in... it's hard for me. To do that, I need you with me. To see your face, to hold you, to know everything's going to be okay."

"I keep feeling," she starts, swiping at her face, "like it's not our time. Like I've been waiting for years and I only get glimpses of it, and we have to fight for every single moment. I just want it to be our time, Tyler. Just once, I want today to be our day."

I tug her against me, dropping my lips to her forehead. "Then let's make today our day."

So, we do.

We stroll LA like tourists.

We laugh and dance and make out like we're in high school.

I have my best friend, the woman who makes me feel more alive than I've ever felt.

I hate letting go of her hand when I drive her to the airport.

Watching her walk away is a million times harder.

I stay at LAX, staring at the departures level until someone honks loudly from behind and I eventually pull out.

On the way back to my place, I roll down the windows.

When I thought of being in LA, staring at the ocean, I dreamed of freedom, but now the air feels colder, and I'm left thinking freedom never felt so lonely before.

Annie

There's nothing like having professionals read—and sing—your script, especially if it's the first time you've heard it out loud.

The SoHo loft is chic and spacious by New York standards. It's still cozy with eight of us sitting in a circle, chairs from the table and stools from the bar pulled around so we're all facing each other.

I've always loved the tradition of a reading. It's like being on stage, nerve-wracking and thrilling at once. It's not unlike reading my poem in front of Carly, though the stakes are much higher. It's personal because my work is personal.

I sit back, pull the pencil from behind my ear, and tap it lightly against my leg as the actors sight-read a song.

The dark-haired woman singing the lead stumbles over a part of the chorus—partly because it's tricky and partly because everyone's flagging a bit after three hours of working on this show.

I hold up a hand. "Let me fix that. Ten-minute break?"

Everyone nods, and I scribble the change I want on her version on the book. If it works, I'll put it into my version, the master.

When I finish, I check my phone. Sure enough, there's a message from my writing partner.

Miranda: How's the reading going?

Annie: A few rough spots. I'll keep you posted. How are you feeling?

Miranda: My body's rebelling. Have a drink for me.

My throat closes up. Her chemo started this week, and she wanted to come today, but I told her to take care of herself.

It's another reminder of how much is riding on this.

A drink appears at my shoulder, and I look up.

"You need a break too," comes a kind, masculine voice.

Jeffrey is tall and pushing sixty-five, with a receding hairline and sharp blue eyes. After reviewing the information on the funders, I knew he was my best chance. The man has three granddaughters and a history of seeing potential in unusual projects.

"This is amazing," I tell him. "Thank you for being so receptive when I asked if we could move the reading to your place. I know Ian usually hosts."

"My pleasure. Can't let him have all the fun. Besides, your pitch was persuasive."

"That's a kind way of saying I showed up at your office unannounced and sang you one of the songs."

His smile is gentle, but his eyes sparkle as he nods toward the balcony. "Let's step outside. It's a nice night."

I follow him out, and he pulls the door shut after us.

"My first musical, we were workshopping it for months," he says under his breath. "Ran three years off-Broadway and—"

"Ten years on it," I finish.

A Broadway show costs millions to stage, and most don't make that back. Then there are the unicorns, the ones that resonate—*Phantom of the*

Opera, Rent, Hamilton. They cover all manner of things, but they stay with us.

"They're not all like that," he goes on at my expression. "A production has to capture people in the right way, at the right time. Most never do that."

"That's why we try. Not because it's easy, but because it's hard." I lean over the railing, staring out at the bright lights of the city as I continue.

"I used to think being in the spotlight was about talent or worthiness or luck. But it's more than that. It's a thousand choices to try something when you're afraid, to say yes when it's easier to say no, to believe in what you're doing on those days you don't believe in yourself.

"Do you believe in this enough to fund this?" I blurt, turning toward him.

His face goes blank, but I'm not here for validation. There's something more I need from him.

"I'm sure people ask you for money every day," I say. "But I'm not asking you to invest in me. I'm asking you to invest in this." I gesture behind me. "This idea, this story, this possibility. If you honestly believe it will move people—that's what we're all trying to do. I know I'm enthusiastic. But don't mistake it for naïve. I've seen a lot of this industry. I understand you need to make a profit. But I also know you wouldn't be in it if there was anything else that would satisfy you."

I take in his impassive face, my hands fisting at my sides as my heart falls into my stomach.

But after a moment, Jeffrey laughs softly. "You must have been influenced by your father."

Once the question, the deflection, would've made me angry. It doesn't anymore. "We're always influenced by the people in our lives."

"Would he be attaching himself to this?"

I shake my head. "I won't ask him, and neither will you. It's not his story."

He turns that over as I stare out over the street, the people laughing and the cabs passing below.

"Well," he says at last, "we'll reserve him tickets."

My glass slips, and I fumble to grab it before it hits the patio. "You mean you'll fund it?" When I look up, he's smiling.

"It's a fabulous story, and I have a couple of directors in mind. But I won't pretend some of the appeal isn't standing right in front of me. Your talent, energy, charm... You'll make a stellar lead."

My heart kicks as I drop into one of the chairs on the balcony.

"Something wrong?" he asks.

"Just waiting for the blood flow to return to my head."

I want to tell Tyler. As the conversation inside drifts through the glass, I want to call him. It's everything I wanted.

But also, it's not.

It's been a week since I came back to New York. Tyler's back in LA now, finalizing the deal on his new house. We left things in a good place but agreed it was best to keep some space between us for a while, which is why I haven't reached out to him and he hasn't reached out to me.

I'm still reliving our time together this summer, the days and nights in Dallas and LA. I decided to write them out like a diary, to preserve them like the perfect memories they are, but every time I start, it's too fresh and it hurts too much, so I close the book.

"Are you all right?"

I blink to see Jeffrey, his glass raised.

"I'm great." I rush to clink my glass to his.

Sadness makes this moment bittersweet. I try to focus on the good, but my heart's still heavy.

"How'd it go?" Elle jumps on me when I enter our apartment. It's two in the morning, and I'm ready to fall into bed, but I give her the news, and she shrieks, wrapping her arms around me. "Shit, A, you're making a show!"

"Apparently." My grin stretches across my tired face.

"So, you did it, and NT wasn't even involved," she

muses. Before I can argue, she heads for the kitchen and pours shots of bourbon. "Cheers."

We toss them back, and the warmth burns down my throat.

I think of Miranda's reaction when I called her on the way home, how ecstatic she'd been despite the late hour. I debated whether to tell her tonight or tomorrow, but hearing her reaction, I was glad I didn't wait.

"You tell Tyler yet?" Elle's gaze over the shot glass is full of meaning.

I shake my head.

"He deserves to know—it's his story too," Elle goes on.

I pour us both another shot and pass her one. "I feel like I pulled it from the air."

We toast and toss this one back too.

"Come on." Elle sets her shot glass on the counter and leans a hip against it, her lips twisting. "A girl who thought her heart was stolen and that's why she couldn't feel goes on a journey with the help of a boy who shows her what it means to live and learns she had it all along."

I'm shaking my head before she finishes. "The female lead is nothing like me. She doesn't have a heart. She doesn't think she's missing anything until someone points that out. I've never had that prob- lem. I feel way too much."

"Obviously. But you're not her. Tyler is."

I wash the shot glasses and cast a look over my shoulder. She tips her chin down, staring at me as if I'm being deliberately slow.

My hands still in the sink, bubbles filling the basin.

"You're the other lead," she goes on. "The boy who shows her what it means to live, and love, and take chances."

I turn off the faucet and watch the water drain out. The shiny dish soap glints on the surface as the bubbles spiral around and around, finally slipping down the drain.

I set the glasses on the drying rack. When I face my roommate, I brace a still-wet hand on the counter. "That's not true."

But my chest squeezes. The next breath is harder than the last.

It's *our* story. Mine and Tyler's. Not all of it of course, but the core.

I cross to the couch and perch on the arm. Elle's face fills with empathy as she follows. "He'd be proud. You should send it to him."

"How long have you known?"

"Since you started telling me about it a year ago. Does he know you love him?"

I shove off the couch and pace the width of our apartment. "Yes." I pause by the window. "But Tyler has always chosen freedom, to do his own thing and rely on himself. New York isn't what he wants. And I want this show, Elle. Not only for me, but also for everyone involved. For everyone who'll get to see it if we keep going."

"You want it enough to let Tyler go? Not that I want to lose you *and* Beck to LA"—her lips curve in a sad smile—"but you could write."

I return to the counter for the shot glasses and pour half a glass more for each of us.

"We always stayed true to our dreams, for better or worse, and I love that about us. But a career isn't made or broken in one perfect moment. It's hundreds of choices over thousands of days. What if love is the same, Elle?" I think of the ups and downs with my family, my dad. "Maybe we were meant to be apart for a couple of years, and that decision wasn't wrong, it was just one more choice that helped us grow and learn and become more of who were supposed to be. Maybe we have more choices ahead of us, starting right now, and nothing in the world can keep us apart if I find ways to choose him."

The ideas start coming in a rush, all at once. "If I can find the right person to play the female lead, I can finish the show without having to be in it."

Her eyes widen. "You'd give up playing the lead for Tyler."

A surge of energy takes me over, and I know in an instant what I'm thinking is right.

"I wouldn't be giving up something I want. I'd be choosing something I don't want to live without."

He's my best friend, the only man I've ever loved.

The only man I *will* love.

Taking up a Broadway stage might have been my dream, but I have another dream that matters every bit as much.

Us.

20

Tyler

I get my bike out to ride to Santa Monica, navigating the ever-present traffic on the way to the address I know by heart.

The property's a house with ocean views—three bedrooms, white stucco, sunshine for days. When I get there, Beck's leaning against his car.

"Nice of 'em to let you come see the place again," my friend comments.

I pass him to get to the door, punching in the code the realtor gave me. "For the price, they should."

I put an offer in last week before the house was scheduled to go on the market, but we built into the conditions that I get another look at it.

He follows me inside.

It's beautiful, open concept with high ceilings.

Too much white, but something tells me that's by design.

I never pictured myself living in something so stunning.

I head through the living room to the patio on the other side, a pool and a deck with a glass wall around it.

"How's it look, pool boy?" Beck laughs.

"It's not bad," I admit, leaning my elbows on the railing.

He takes up a post next to me, sliding his aviator sunglasses off the top of his head and up his nose. "Why do you look so bummed? There are a dozen reasons to be satisfied this week." He counts them on his fingers. "I have a ten-episode series coming to a streaming network near you. You got your dream house, and Annie got her show funded."

I jerk upright, whirling to face him so fast he jumps.

"What did you say?"

A guilty expression crosses my friend's face. "You didn't know."

My hearts aches. "No."

Because we decided not to talk for a while, I remind myself. It was mutual. *So, why does it feel like shit?*

Since she left, I've been trying not to think about her, but I can't help it. I'm going about my life, but I see her on street corners, I picture her smile at night, I hear her voice whispering in my ear.

When I went on tour, I promised I wouldn't look her up on social.

I've stuck to that now, too.

But I keep looking at the photo of us in that bar in Dallas.

It's not cheating to stare at the curves of her lips in that picture, to remember how it felt to have her next to me.

I turn to head inside, Beck's footsteps at my back as I wander through the kitchen. Even the microwave is a stainless steel thing of beauty.

You could make some bitchin' Rice Krispies squares.

I pull on a drawer, then let it slide back in on its special hinges.

Something occurs to me. "Just tell me that douche NT isn't the one funding her show."

Beck laughs, but there's a hint of sadness underneath as he tugs on the door of the fridge to inspect the inside, sliding the sunglasses down his nose to peer overtop. "You heard about Elle's nickname."

"What does it mean?"

"Elle called him Not Tyler from the time they started dating because she knew anyone who wasn't you wouldn't measure up."

Forget shutting out the pain. It washes over me in a wave.

I cross to the glass doors again, pressing my nose and forehead against the smooth surface as I shut my eyes. It'll probably leave marks.

I give zero fucks.

"I wanted to be with her, Beck," I bite out through my clenched jaw. "So fucking much."

He snorts. "The Tyler from Vanier wouldn't have stood by and watched his girl walk away."

I fold my arms over my chest. "The Tyler from Vanier was volatile. All I could think about was getting out from under the weight of my dad, his resentment."

"But you've let it go. The past is the past. The things you were, the things you wanted... you don't owe them anything. That includes this dream of hiding out here alone in the sunshine."

"It wasn't about hiding out. I wanted to fix my hand, get another album done, and buy my security. It was about—"

"Freedom? How's that feel? Without the people you love, freedom's pretty fucking quiet, Ty."

Silence hangs between us.

"I have you."

"I won't fuck you."

"Pretty sure you grabbed my ass once when you were drunk."

"More than once," he concedes. "But I wouldn't try anything because you and my Manatee... you're it. What we all want. I know New York's cold with a lot of memories, but you gotta see both sides."

I arch a brow.

"You could be cold outside in New York or cold inside in LA."

I stare at my palm, the web of scars on it.

"A long time ago, this girl told me I had a bright future because of my fate line," I say. "I can't see it anymore, bright or not."

Despite the heaviness in my chest, I won't be the same man I was, and it's not just because of what happened two years ago. It's because of Annie. She's made me better, more caring and considerate.

Like music, she opened me up. Because of her, I'm the kind of person with friends I count on and who count on me. I have people like Jax looking out for me, kids like Shay who look up to me.

I couldn't have tolerated it, not to mention sought it out. Once, letting people in was like being scorched by the hot sun.

But every day, Annie exposed me to her brightness, whether I wanted her to or not. And eventually, I stopped turning away from it and started turning toward it. "And it's a problem that your life's not what you expected?" Beck asks.

"No." Conviction grows deep in my gut. "It's not."

I'll always love her, but I want more than a fucking feeling. I want to be with her. I want a front-row seat to every success and failure she has for the rest of our lives.

My phone buzzes and I glance at it.

It's an email from Annie with an attachment.

I click it open, zoom in on the lines of the script.

"What are you—"

I hold up a hand at Beck as I read the first scene.

Then I drop onto the couch and scan the second.

After the third I jump up, heading for the door.

"Where are you going?" Beck calls, emerging from the back of the house.

I snap my head up and head for the front door. "There's somewhere I need to be."

Beck points back toward the rest of the house. "But you haven't checked out my future bedroom."

"I asked for avocado," Zeke tells the waitress on the patio that afternoon. His voice is cordial, but his eyes narrow as he squints against the sun.

She disappears through the doors of the restaurant, past the palm trees blowing in the breeze.

"Hard to get everything you want, isn't it?" Zeke leans forward over the table between us.

"It doesn't have to be."

He grins. "The guys said you were at the studio yesterday with some suggestions on the tracks. Glad you're coming around. You can meet marketing next week."

I stare at the burger in front of me, waiting for his food to return. *Fuck it.* I take a mouthful of mine.

After swallowing the first bite, I say, "I'm meeting them right after this."

Zeke's brows shoot up in surprise. "I'm pleased to see you're enthusiastic."

"That's not the word I'd use. I'm leaving LA and I don't want any talk that I'm not fulfilling my contract."

He laughs. "You're not leaving LA. You just got back."

I mentally review the points that came together quickly once I'd decided on my next move. "I know I haven't been the easiest to work with, but that's going to change. You'll still have input on the songs and production for the rest of the album. But I will record it at the studio of my choosing."

Zeke shifts back in his chair, folding his arms, but I'm not done.

"I will commit to being a better collaborator. Including paying for someone at the label to coordinate promotion, which, as we've established, isn't my strength. In return, what I do on my own time is my own business. It won't compromise the label or its brand."

"Tyler. This is impossible."

"The word you're looking for is 'unorthodox,'" I supply. "The label's ownership is in this to make money. You saw that in me. You gave me a chance and it paid off. Now I'm offering you a chance. If you don't like it, you can sue me for breach of contract, which will be time consuming and expensive and make us both less valuable."

He blinks at me. "Is that all?"

His voice makes it clear he thinks I've lost my mind.

I rise from my chair and toss a fifty on the table for my half-finished burger. "A summary of what I'm proposing is in your email. You can send me any comments over the next forty-eight hours. After my surgery, I'm leaving town."

I start for the door, but Zeke calls after me. "Where are you going?"

I heave out a breath. "Where I should've been all along."

* * *

The door opens to reveal screaming children and a tired-looking thirty-something woman who straightens in recognition when she sees me.

I rub a hand over my neck. "I'm looking for Jax."

"He's in the yard. Are there any more musicians coming?" she calls after me hopefully as I head through the house, a sprawling, new-looking ranch that's not as big as Jax's but still screams money.

It's been two days since my hand surgery, and though the surgeon said it went well, it's too soon to know if this will make the difference I'm hoping for by taking away most of the pain and stiffness.

But no matter what happens, for the first time, I'm not lying awake at night, willing this to be the thing that fixes me.

As I head out the back doors and into a sprawling yard filled with bright colors, children's entertainment, and clusters of adults, I don't have to ask where to find Jax—it's clear from all the moms staring at him. He's in one corner, talking to a man who looks like the only other dad here.

When Jax looks up and sees me, it's his turn to do a double take.

I shouldn't have shown up in Dallas unannounced, but it was a good thing Jax wasn't home when I got there. That gave me more time to get ready for what I have to say.

"Haley said I'd find you here," I say when I pull up next to him.

"Usually Hales does party duty, but she's still on bed rest."

The other man takes Jax's stare as his cue to leave, and I swallow my amusement as I look across the sprawling yard with a jungle gym, a gated-off pool, a bouncy castle, and tables with snacks and desserts. "How many kids come to these things?"

"Too many."

It takes me a moment to spot Sophie at the top of the slide in overalls and a lime-green T-shirt, her hair in pigtails with matching green ribbons. She's not looking for her dad. She's focused on the ride she's on, and her face splits with a smile as she slides down to the bottom, bumping into the last kid—who failed to clear the landing zone in time—with a little shriek.

The woman who answered the door approaches, her gaze moving between us. "Would you like a hat?"

"Love one. Jax too."

I take two party hats from her and hold one out for Jax. He shoves his hands in his pockets.

"Please say you came to relieve me," he states when she's gone.

"I did come to tell you something, but it might not be a relief." I take a breath. "I'm going to marry your daughter."

Jax stiffens, his gaze never leaving the throng of kids on the jungle gym. Sophie chases another kid, running under the slide and lunging. "Sophie's a little young."

"I'm serious. I'm in love with Annie. I have been since before I knew what that meant. She fucking loves me too."

A little boy whose shoe fell off as he tried to dash past us looks up from refastening the Velcro, eyes round with delight. Then he takes off toward his parents, hollering.

"She'll always be yours, and I'm not trying to take her away from you," I go on. "But she'll always be mine too."

Jax rubs a hand over his square jaw. "And if I don't accept that?"

My body stiffens as I turn the paper hat in my hands.

"You're the closest thing I've had to a father. You trusted me and let me into your family. But if you're going to make me choose, Jax—I choose her."

The truth of those words rings through me. I choose Annie over certainty, over safety, over money, over fame. No life I could lead is as full without her, and if being with her means putting everything I am, everything I've been, on the line? I'm ready to do it. For now and for always.

"What about your contract?" Jax asks.

"Zeke and I came to an agreement for how I'll finish the album. I also committed to more public appearances, and paying for a PR rep on the label's staff since I don't do enough 'fan engagement', in his words."

"I'm impressed. Did you negotiate that collaboratively or drop an ultimatum on his desk?"

"Something in between."

Jax stares me down. "Listen to me, Tyler."

I wait him out, my breathing steady, prepared for whatever he's about to say.

He takes the party hat still in his hands and sets it on my head, snapping the elastic down around my chin. "If you marry my daughter, I'm not taking your kids to any fucking birthday parties."

21

Annie

"Here we go," I say as the woman I've been on the phone trying to land for the last few days takes the stage for her audition.

Jeffrey's on one side of me, Miranda on the other. I don't look over to see their reactions while the actress performs the song we sent her.

But I'm sitting bolt upright.

She's good—really good.

When she wraps up, we thank her, and she heads out of the theater.

"We're screwed." Miranda Talbot's blunt tone has me cutting her a look after the actress is gone.

"What do you mean? She was great."

"She wasn't right," Jeffrey agrees.

My stomach flips. "Come on. She's a household

name. I bent over backward to get her"—even using one of my dad's contacts, which I'd decided was worth it given the circumstances—"and she'll definitely get the show attention."

We've been running auditions at a small off-Broadway theater all day to cast the main roles for our show. Even Miranda refused to miss this, insisting the worst of the reaction from her most recent chemo session was over and tearing up a few headshots from wannabe actors would help her feel better anyway.

"It's a no," Jeffrey says crisply, glancing my way.

"We've identified great people for four characters," I point out.

"But not the leads."

"There's another group after lunch, right?" I ask our production assistant.

She shakes her head.

Shit. "I could've sworn there were more…" I riffle through the papers in front of me.

Jeffrey sighs. He's done this a dozen times before, but I can tell he's disappointed. "We don't have a lead, we don't have a show. Frankly, I'm concerned you're in such a hurry to distance yourself from it."

"It's not that. I love this show more than I thought I'd love anything," I promise. "But there's something —*someone*—I love even more."

His face unreadable, he gets up and reaches for

his phone, hitting a contact as he heads down the aisle.

We've thrown ourselves into preparing for this.

I figured today would be more like a victory lap, but it's turning out to be hell. *How can it be so hard to find the right person?*

"Knock, knock." Elle sticks her head in the door before coming into the theater bearing a brown paper bag.

"Is that something to numb the pain?" Miranda asks dryly as Elle stops next to our row.

"Hoagies," my roommate explains.

"That'll work."

"You want Annie's too?" Elle asks, passing them out. "She likes the pain. It's cleansing."

I shoot my friend side-eye. My phone buzzes, and I glance at it. There's a text from my dad, and the tension in my chest eases just a little.

I walk toward a dark corner and hit his contact, and he picks up on a video call.

"Thought you had auditions this weekend," he says.

"We do. We're at a theater right now." I flip him around to see the space, then back to see me. "Unfortunately, we haven't found the right actors yet."

He frowns. "Don't give up. Sometimes the best things come from the last place you expect. Like Tyler finding Shay. Her single releases next week."

"That's great, Dad." I swallow. "Have you talked to Tyler? I sent him something a few days ago, and I hoped I'd hear back by now."

My dad's expression shifts, and I can't read the strange look on his face. "I think he misses you."

The backs of my eyes burn, and I'm glad I'm in a dark corner. "I miss him too. Well, I should get back to it."

Dad nods. "We're proud of you. All of us. Let us know how your casting goes."

"I will."

I hang up and head back toward Miranda, who has already unwrapped a sandwich and is in conversation with Elle.

"I want to do this show where the audience sits on stage and I'm watching them from the floor," Elle's saying, and Miranda's studying her with a raised brow.

They both look at me when I return, and Jeffrey comes back down the aisle.

"We have one more to see."

"Who?" I ask, frowning. Every headshot in front of me is familiar. We've seen each of these people on stage already today.

But Elle stiffens next to me, grabbing my arm. "Holy shit."

Someone walks past us up the aisle. I lift my head slowly, tingles starting low in my stomach and spreading to my arms, my legs, my toes.

The man takes the stairs to the stage as if this were his house, not an audition. He's confident, relaxed, in dark jeans and a shirt rolled up at the sleeves to reveal swirls of black ink.

Tyler hits center stage and turns to face us. I'm so floored it takes a moment for me to catch up when his gaze meets mine.

Jeffrey shifts into the seat next to me. "Well?"

I blink. "Well what?"

"Go with him."

I shift out of my seat, nearly forgetting the book before I trip toward the stage, take the steps, and cross to Tyler. I stop in front of him.

Even under the lights, he takes up the stage, takes up the room.

"What are you doing?" I shake my head in disbelief. I'm so happy he's here I almost don't want to know the answer.

"I'm auditioning. You sent me a script."

My jaw hits the floor. "I wanted you to read it. I wasn't asking you to audition."

His mouth twitches. "You should've been more specific."

"But..." My mouth works, nothing coming out. "You can't be auditioning on Broadway."

"Someone told me you don't need your hands to

make good music. That it can come from your head and your heart."

Tyler cuts an expectant look toward my colleagues. Jeffrey folds his arms, and Miranda smiles broader than I've seen her smile since I returned from Dallas.

Tyler nods to the pianist in the corner, who plays the arrangement. The song moves through me, the accompaniment to the song I spent this summer writing.

Tyler sings the first part of the duet, and I melt into the floor.

I can't move.

Can't think.

Can't breathe.

Can't live.

Except I am living, and his voice, his presence, is the only thing responsible for it.

Music is a language that makes sense when all the others don't. And right now, there's no greater expression of life's promise than what's happening around me, inside me.

Hearing Tyler as the dreamer makes my heart explode. I almost miss jumping in at the female lead's part, but once I do, I focus on the song and match him tone for tone, measure for measure, phrase for phrase.

Every verse and chorus I'm vibrating, caught

between the stage and the words and the man in front of me.

When we finish, the final notes of our voices and the piano fading, Jeffrey, Miranda and Elle are all standing silently.

They don't need to say it was good.

Because it wasn't good.

It was *right*.

It was everything.

Jeffrey's the first to move, nodding. "Tyler. You understand we're looking to do previews in three months, then move it to off-Broadway with an initial twelve-month run."

"I have other commitments, but I can fit them around this."

I'm still trying to catch up. "You'd have to move back to New York. You hate New York."

"I can't hate it. It has you." My heart expands.

"Good. We have a show," Jeffrey says.

"I have a condition," Tyler interjects. "Annie has to do it with me."

I can barely breathe through the tightness in my throat. "It's our show. It always has been. But I've been trying to find the right people to play the leads so I didn't have to be in it. So I could be in LA with you."

His forehead presses to mine, and I reach up to tug on his hair, at a loss for words.

"If it's our story, it seems fair we should do it. At least for the initial run."

I shake my head. "But what about your record deal? The house in LA?"

"I withdrew the offer. And I've pulled some strings with the label to give me more flexibility."

"You really want to do this," I whisper.

"I really do. Just tell me one thing—why'd you give them this ending?"

"Because if I got to create my own world... we'd be together in it. Every single time."

My gaze falls to his mouth, his full lips, and I need them on me.

Tyler kisses me, and it's everything—we're everything.

A throat clearing has me pulling back before I can do something about it—Miranda.

Elle's devouring a sandwich, eyes glued to the stage, and even our funder looks entertained.

"If you'll excuse me, I have some calls to make about marketing. This"—Jeffrey nods to us—"I can sell."

My stomach flips as I take Tyler in again, the rest of the room falling away.

There's a tic in his jaw, and he looks hesitant for the first time since he got here. "The ring I gave you —do you still have it?"

I reach into my neckline and pull out the chain,

the ring I've been wearing since I returned to New York dangling on the end.

"That's from our past. I have something to give you for our future. And I want a future with you. I even talked to your dad about it."

So that's why Dad was acting so weird on the phone. "I bet that was interesting."

Tyler chuckles softly. "I told him I'm never letting you go again, and if he has a problem with it, he can go through me."

He reaches into his pocket and produces a box.

My heart hammers against my back, and I'm feeling lightheaded.

Then he kneels.

I've always felt at my most powerful and powerless on a stage, but this moment with Tyler Adams on his knees for me puts every other moment to shame.

"Annie, you've always been the best part of my life. Even when I tried not to let you in, you were there. So bright, so damned fresh, and you believed in me when no one did. When I didn't."

His beautiful voice cracks, and I'm trembling from his words, from anticipation of what he'll say next.

"I might have come from nothing, but I've been around the damned world. Which means I can say without a doubt that you are the best part of it, Six. I know we both have dreams, but mine aren't worth living unless I can live them with you."

He flips the lid on the box, and the sparkling contents almost blind me.

"I've never loved anyone the way I love you. I will do whatever it takes to convince you to spend your life with me.

"I'll trade you. The old ring for a new one."

It's gorgeous, reflecting every bit of light in this space, shining every emotion in his eyes back at me.

"No."

Tyler's face tightens in alarm. "No what?"

I rush on. "No, I won't give you the old ring back. Because our past is part of us.

"But you're my best friend. The only boy I ever loved. The person who challenges me, who's there for me, who makes me feel like I am everything I ever need to be. So I guess I could marry you."

Tyler's face is so full of fierceness I could explode.

He slips the ring onto my finger, and it feels like forever.

Then he rises, grabbing me again in a kiss that's hot enough I might melt onto this stage.

"Jewelry whore!"

I reluctantly tear my lips from Tyler's and cut a look toward Elle in the audience.

"You trying to steal my roomie, Adams?" she calls.

"It's done." I love the satisfaction in his tone, the possessiveness.

"I love you so damned much."

My blood heats. "I love you too."

Something lands on the stage, and I realize it's a sock.

"For your bedroom door," Elle tosses as she turns back up the aisle with a wave.

Tyler's grin is delicious. "Tell me we're done here."

I meet Miranda's gaze. "I think we've accomplished what we set out to."

"Agreed," my mentor says. "Annie, we'll talk tomorrow. Congratulations, Mr. Adams. And I don't mean about the role." She smiles and turns to head out.

I don't get to see her leave because Tyler's yanking me against him.

"Come here," he murmurs against my lips.

Then he's kissing me, and my brows shoot up my face.

But I wrap my arms around his neck and kiss him back with everything in me.

I'm here on a damned New York stage, and all I care about is the man holding me, the one who's always held me up, always made me feel like enough.

Like we're enough.

And despite how far we've come, something tells me we're only getting started.

22

___

Annie

I wake up in the morning, and the bed smells like Tyler.

I roll over to find him gone, but there's a sticky note on the pillow.

Morning, Six.

I grin as I shift out of bed, tugging down the hem of my T-shirt and stepping around the overnight bag he brought. I head out to the living room.

"This for me?" I hold up the sticky note.

Tyler turns from where he's standing at the counter, the smell of coffee wafting through our place. "Mhmm. How'd I know you'd have the ingredients for Rice Krispies squares?"

"It's a bribe, isn't it?" I shift in front of him, winding my arms around his neck. "So I don't tell my dad I woke up in your bed." I cock my head. "Okay, technically my bed. But still."

His hands slide down my sides, making every part of me wake up under his touch even before he presses his lips to my jaw. "You're going to wake up in my bed every day, always."

He hitches me up on the counter and kisses me, taking his time. I press myself against him, threading my hands into his hair. He tugs me closer to the edge, my panties the only thing between us.

And they're getting damp fast.

"Elle could walk in," I protest half-heartedly.

"Elle's out for the day," Tyler mutters between kisses. "And we have to make up for lost time. I'm going to have you on every surface of this apartment."

Holy.

His fingers trace a path up the inside of my thigh, and I hiccup a breath when they slip under my panties and tease me.

"Oh."

"Oh what?"

"Ohhh, I've missed that."

He chuckles before pressing two fingers inside

me. My nails dig into his shoulders as my body contracts around him.

"You're so wet. Think I'm going to slide right in."

"Do it," I mumble.

Tyler works off his jeans, no boxer briefs underneath. He's already impressively hard, his abs flexing as if it takes all of him not to impale me right now. He pulls me to the edge of the counter, brushing his tip against my needy skin.

I kiss him with love, with need, with the desperation that never seems to be far away when it comes to us... but with a kind of comfort that's new.

We have nothing but time.

Tyler eases into me as if he believes that too. I'm balanced on the edge of the counter, my legs tight around him, holding on to keep from falling in more ways than one.

"Nothing's has ever felt as good as you," he murmurs against my mouth. "You're made for me, Annie."

Every stroke is beautiful satisfaction and torture at once, and I need more. He rasps as he builds us both up, fingers digging into my ass as he fucks me.

It's beautiful. It's messy. It's us.

When I come around him, he can't hold back, and he comes too, groaning his release against my shoulder while my fingers play in his hair, the last of the aftershocks running through me.

"Well, I feel better," I murmur.

He grins. "Same."

"Good, because we have a busy day."

"We do?"

"I have to do work things."

"You can't take today off? Because I'm going to need you again in two hours max."

Arousal washes over me. "No. But you can come with me. Maybe we can fit in a quickie at lunch."

"'Bring your fiancé to work' day. Sold."

I bite my cheek because the thought of bringing Tyler to my anything as my fiancé makes me so insanely happy.

"Tell me you're done by five," Tyler says.

I trace his handsome jaw with a finger. "Should be possible. Why?"

"Because I have a realtor lined up to show us a couple places. I love Elle too, but we can't live here long term."

"The rent is great."

"I don't care. I'm getting us something nice for as long as we're in New York."

"Fine. Are you going to record here?"

"I thought I might get involved in your dad's label. Both as a business proposition and for my own music. But only if it won't come between you."

I shake my head. "Not at all. He'd love that. And I would too."

Something buzzes from across the room—my phone.

"Shit. It's Dad."

We didn't call him back after getting engaged last night because we wanted a few moments to ourselves.

"He knows you're here. If I don't answer, he's going to think we were having sex."

Tyler's eyes crinkle at the corners. "Please don't answer."

I pull down my T-shirt and straighten my hair. Then I squeeze past him and grab the phone, sliding the bar so the video call connects.

"Hey, you guys!" I say but frown as I take in the unfamiliar backdrop, my dad's pale face, and Haley's sweaty one. "Did you paint? Oh my God! You're in the hospital. You had the baby!"

"Once we finally got here, he was out in three hours," Haley sighs.

Tyler appears behind me, and my dad's eyes narrow while Haley looks delighted, the baby in her arms.

We gush over baby Mason and get all the details.

"Nice work," Tyler says, and my dad grins.

He looks beyond proud. "How about you two? Any news we should know?"

"Well, we cast someone in the lead for the musical."

I swear my dad looks disappointed. "Thats it?"

"And..." I hold up the ring.

"Tyler. Tell me you didn't go down on one knee," Dad snorts.

Haley shoves his shoulder. "Don't act like you're too cool for that. You've done it. You even cried."

My jaw drops.

"I didn't cry," he says.

"Your eyes were shining."

"Trick of the light."

"Anyway." Haley rolls her eyes, turning back to us. "We're so happy for you both."

"Thanks Haley, we're happy for you, too. All of you."

Tyler clears his throat. "Jax, we have a couple of weeks before we really gear up for the musical. I'd like to use your studio if I can book time."

"You got it."

When we hang up and I toss the phone back on the table, feeling the only man I've ever loved pull me against him again, I've never been more content.

"I'm ready for those Rice Krispies squares now," I sigh.

Tyler's eyes crinkle. "Only if I can eat them off you."

Tyler

"It's gone. It's actually gone," Annie mutters, lifting pillows to search the couch in our living room.

I roll up the cuffs on my dress shirt as I cross the bright, airy apartment from the master bedroom. "Six, tell me you haven't lost your ring."

She crosses to me, her face a mask of shock.

Then she pulls her hand out to show me the diamond glinting on her finger.

Relief slams into me, along with pleasure.

Every time I see it on her hand, I feel that way. Even though we've been engaged for three months, I haven't gotten over knowing she's mine.

Beck teases that it won't go away until she's signed the certificate and she can't back out.

The truth is I know it won't go away even after that.

"Why do you look so happy?" Annie asks, planting a hand on her hip.

I tear my gaze away from her teasing face to take her in, from her purple-painted toenails to her long legs to the curve of her hips, the dip of her waist, and the valley between her breasts, all outlined by the tidy black dress.

It should be cute.

It's not. It makes me want to drag her against me and do unspeakable things to her.

"Because you're marrying me."

Her eyes darken, and she tucks a piece of the hair she finished curling in our huge en suite bathroom an hour ago behind her ear. "But I can't find my phone, and how the hell am I supposed to buzz people up?"

"I'll call it in a second. We'll find it."

I back her toward the windows, and her eyes widen. "Tyler, we have guests arriving any minute."

"You already lost the phone. Can't buzz them up. Let's call it off."

Her back meets the window, and she sucks in a breath.

I drop my mouth to her neck, loving her soft floral scent and the way she arches, offering up more of her—all of her.

I'll devour every inch.

"We can't call it off," she pants even though her fingers thread into my hair. "It's our engagement-previews-housewarming party."

"Fuck it. They'll just bring booze and say how happy they are for us. I can tell you how happy I am for us."

My hand sneaks under the hem of her dress and under the scrap of lace she calls panties.

"You're so wet," I tell her as if she doesn't know. "How long have you been like this?"

"Since you walked out wearing that shirt I bought you."

"Why's that?"

"Because I like knowing I get to dress you. You're like my own broody rock star Ken doll."

I sink two fingers into her in retaliation, and she moans, squirming.

"We'll have lots of time for that when we're married," Annie protests, but I know she's joking because her hips lift to meet every stroke of my hand.

I glance at the clock. "We have at least ten minutes."

Annie's lips curve. "Well, in that case."

I fuck her against the floor-to-ceiling windows.

I will never, ever get tired of her sounds, the way she feels around me.

This woman owns me.

She's built me up, made me more than I thought I could be.

And everything I am, everything I will ever be, I'd give it to her.

I didn't think it was possible to love another person the way I love her, but she's shown me giving your heart can be worth it if you give it to the right person.

When we finish, we clean up quickly and track down her phone before our guests start arriving.

"This building is beautiful, Annie. I swear the entire thing is windows. And you!" Haley gushes as we open the door to the hallway, Sophie bounding beside her. Jax has the baby carrier in his arms.

"You're glowing," Haley goes on as she steps inside.

Annie's face goes red. "Thanks." She passes me the huge flower arrangement Haley gives her. "Can you take these to the dining room?"

"Sure." But I can't resist brushing my lips over her ear. "I love that *now* you're blushing when I was inside you ten minutes ago against those windows."

And as I head for the kitchen without waiting for her response, I love that I'll be inside her tonight after everyone goes home, that I'm the one who gets to make this beautiful, strong woman soft.

Over the next hour, everyone filters in and mingles around our new apartment.

Elle's here, plus Rae, plus Pen, and Beck. Elle catches us up on her stand-up performances and the news that she's made it to the third round of a nationwide comic breakout competition. Rae's been DJ-ing in New York and Miami but made sure she could be here for our party.

Even Beck's sister, Serena, came since she lives in New York, with her boyfriend, Wes.

"Holy shit," Wes states, unselfconscious as he takes in the views. "How big is this place?"

"Two thousand square feet," I supply.

"My bedroom could fit in your bathroom," Rae deadpans.

Annie doesn't feel badly in the slightest. "Hey, that was my bedroom," she points out to the woman who took over her spot in Elle's apartment when Annie moved out.

"This is what Broadway money buys you," Beck jokes. "And you've only started previews for the show."

In reality, a good part of our income is from my royalties. The new album I'm finishing contains the best music I've made to date.

The surgery helped with the pain in my hand, but not my ability to play guitar.

Still, I care less than I used to. Annie helped me

realize I can write amazing music and let other people help me perform it.

Serena laughs and shoves at her brother. "You can't talk. I have people texting me photos of you from online magazines every other week naming you the hottest new actor in Hollywood."

"Hottest," he points out with a grin. "Not richest."

His show started releasing weekly last month, and it's all anyone can talk about. It's all but guaranteed to get renewed for a second season.

Annie sneaks up on me with a glass of champagne.

I make a face at the drink. "Do I have to?" I joke as I take it from her.

"I know you hate bubbles. But Dad wants to make a toast." She smiles.

Annie and her dad are back on solid ground, and it seems I'm in his good graces, too.

I think he has finally appreciated what I learned a long time ago—Annie's going to do whatever she wants, and she'll probably crush it, too. I don't need to protect her from the industry.

If anything, we should protect the industry from her, as evidenced by the fact that she's dragged a show from practically conception to previews—with her and me in the leading roles—in less than three years.

"Is everyone here?" she asks me. "What about your friend from London?"

I invited a couple of guys I met on tour and stayed in touch with off and on. Annie's been excited to meet them.

There's a knock at the door. "That must be him," I tell her. "Apparently they don't have clocks in the UK."

I go to open it, expecting to see Harry's tall, broad frame.

But instead of Harry, it's a giant ice sculpture on a dolly with a uniformed delivery man.

"Mr. Adams? Mr. King sends his regards."

The delivery guy wheels the sculpture in, and Annie has him put it in the center of our marble kitchen island.

"What kind of a man sends an ice sculpture?" Rae muses, fascinated.

"Let me call him." I go to our balcony, stepping out onto the long patio and hitting his number.

He answers on the fourth ring. "Yeah."

"It's Tyler. What the hell happened? Are you coming to the party?"

In truth, I don't care so much about the party, but it's odd of him to not do what he says he will.

There's a groan and some cursing, as if he bumped into something. "You haven't heard."

His voice is so dead I'm worried. I google his name. "Jesus. Are you alright?"

I see page after page of articles on my real estate and entertainment mogul friend, and his girlfriend—now ex-girlfriend—going off the deep end after they broke up.

"Swearing off women for life," he vows.

"Hang in there. I'll call you tomorrow."

I click off, trying not to let worry set in. Harry wouldn't have been at the helm of a massive empire without having his shit together. Hell, he's one of the people whose advice helped me get through life on tour.

I owe him one.

But for now, I push it from my mind and head back to the living room.

"Everything okay?" Annie asks when I rejoin her.

"Yeah, nothing to worry about." I brush my lips across her cheek.

Glasses clink, and we all look up from where we're standing to see Jax holding up his champagne and looking slightly uncomfortable.

"This is a strange day. It would be normal to feel as if I have two children starting their lives." We all look at the baby and Sophie, who's swinging her legs on the couch. "But it feels as if four of my children are."

Annie's hand squeezes mine hard, and I swallow.

"I'm blessed to have the people I have, and I don't know what I've done to deserve it. But I know Tyler and Annie deserve each other."

By the end of the toast, Annie's in tears and Haley's smiling so broadly it looks as if it might crack her face.

I drink my champagne, and for once, I don't even mind the fucking bubbles.

My fiancée goes to hug her dad, and when he pulls back, he looks at me.

"We have a little something special planned," I say.

A buzz starts as I go to our second bedroom—a music room now—to retrieve the guitar Annie bought me, plus my second favorite.

I pass the latter to Jax, and we do a song together.

Everyone listens and cheers when it's over.

"What are you guys doing for your wedding?" Elle asks after we've finished a drink and cake and Sophie's taken off around the apartment to run the perimeter, trailing a finger along the ornate baseboards.

Annie and I exchange a look.

"We were thinking somewhere warm," she says, shooting me a smile.

Haley shifts forward, beaming. "LA?"

"An island," I say. "Of course, you're all invited."

Cheers go up.

"What's that look on your face?" Annie murmurs much later, once everyone's gone home except Jax and Haley and the kids in the guest bedroom.

It's just the two of us on the balcony, and I pull her against me.

"I'm happy," I admit, brushing a curl out of her face as I drink in the sight of her warm eyes, the curve of her lips. "So fucking happy, Annie. Everything we've been through came full circle for me today. It reminded me this is what it's like to have family. And I'm not afraid anymore. Whatever happens, we've got it covered."

"Even a new album and a Broadway show and…" she trails off, brows lifting in mock horror, "an island wedding?" she teases.

I drag her mouth to mine, kissing her breathless before I pull back.

"Can't wait."

I hope you loved the conclusion of Tyler and Annie's story. For an extra dose of this angsty power couple… join my VIP List and read an EXCLUSIVE Rivals holiday story now!

https://claims.prolificworks.com/free/9ItBACwD

Old friends, new enemies, entertainment's brightest rising stars and biggest egos - together for the destination wedding of the decade.
What could possibly go wrong?

So many readers asked me about Tyler and Annie's wedding. If you're still craving more angsty, addictive rock star deliciousness...**pick up A Love Song for Always today!**

NEXT UP FOR TYLER AND ANNIE...

Read a short excerpt below

CHAPTER ONE

Annie

Seven days until the wedding

"Can't we move any faster?" I lean toward the partition between the front and back seats of the limo. "There must be another road. Let me check."

The driver shoots me a patient look. "Miss Jamieson, it's the 405."

From the seat next to me, Rae laughs silently. "Forgive her. She has a serious case of Tyler Adams withdrawal caused by spending too much time apart from her hot fiancé."

Since I jumped out of bed in New York this morning ahead of the five-thirty alarm to shower and dress, every part of me has been buzzing with anticipation.

Most of my day was spent on the flight to LA with Rae, but I was too distracted to work or read.

Now, the stop-and-go traffic makes me want to roll down my window and shout at the world. Instead, I drum my fingers on the bare knee I nicked my second time over it with a razor.

"Seriously. I don't need to crash with you and Tyler while I play my gigs this week," Rae goes on.

"Yes, you do. There are five bedrooms." Tyler took me on a virtual tour before he rented the house before our wedding. It gave him a home base to work on album release promotions with the studio until I could hand my Broadway role to another actress so Tyler and I could have the next month together before his tour. "Even when Dad and Haley show up with the kids tomorrow, that leaves plenty of space."

Traffic breaks, and the car surges toward the exit.

Yes.

"Did you see the news about Wicked Records?" Rae holds up an article on her phone about my Dad's former label.

I resolve to focus and not degenerate into a throbbing ball of need now that my fiancé is only minutes away.

"Sounds like after years of mismanagement, they're going down fast. Dad hasn't been involved with them for a long time. Not since he was fighting over his songs."

"Have he or your stepmom said anything?"

"Not to me." But we haven't exchanged more than a rushed voicemail or emails with wedding logistics in the better part of a month given how busy things have been preparing for this time off.

My finger drumming on my knee starts again.

"Just as well you're dropping me at the club so I won't be there when you see Tyler," Rae offers. "I don't want to be within earshot when you guys... *reunite*." She enunciates each syllable.

There's no point trying to hide the flush that crawls up my face.

I have been anticipating all the parts of seeing my fiancé. Not only because we're getting married in a week, but because I haven't kissed him, touched him, or shared more than a sexy FaceTime call with him in a month.

I've been in love with Tyler Adams for a decade, long before he became a rock star and I wrote a Broadway show.

Now we're about to tie the knot.

The obstacles that kept us apart felt insurmountable at the time. But our love, our tenacity, and maybe a little destiny kept bringing us back to one another. Next weekend is validation of all we've been through.

"I grew up wanting to be on stage, but the whole bride fantasy skipped me," I admit.

"No parade with stuffed animals down a made-up aisle?"

I shake my head. "But the moment Tyler and I decided on a date, it was like something took me over. I wanted all of it. The guests. The dress. The cake. The music."

"The man," she finishes.

And what a man.

I swore I'd never fall for a rock star. Growing up with my dad's fame rubbed me the wrong way. I felt I had to prove myself—to him and to everyone. It took years for me to realize I belonged, that I could carve my own path without being lessened by his or jealous of Tyler's relationship with my dad.

"Our lives have been anything but perfect. This week will be the exception," I confide.

Our destination wedding will take place on a stunning island with private beaches and exquisite accommodations. After, Tyler and I have cleared our schedules for nearly a month. There'll be nothing but relaxation and enjoy newly wedded bliss with my best friend, who also happens to be my fiancé and the hottest guy on the planet.

I've been planning it with crazed fervor.

To be clear, perfect doesn't mean glossy-magazine-worthy. It's about having time with each other and the people we love in a beautiful, private place that feels like heaven.

The car pulls up at the club, and Rae gets out before leaning in the open window. "Do me a favor and put a sock on the door if you're not done when I get back."

"Does anyone even own socks in LA?" But I wave, and the car pulls off again.

As we take the streets up into the Hills, excitement thrums low in my stomach. Tyler's been finishing his album to earn the month off for our wedding before he goes on tour. Even while living together in New York for most of a year, I didn't feel as though we had time together because we were doing eight shows a week. It was a thrilling and exhausting grind, but we decided to move him out of the lead role a few months after it started on Broadway so he could finish his album.

Now I want him to myself.

I check my phone for Tyler's texts from when I left this morning.

Annie: Can't wait to see you.

Tyler: Can't wait to taste you.

My thighs press together under my short, black dress. I could text Tyler to say we're a few minutes away.

But that would ruin the surprise.

Instead, I put on a song from his new album. His voice wraps around me, raw and sexy and the kind of earnest that makes fans go crazy.

By the time the driver pulls up, passing two parked Rolls and a Maserati on the road before turning into the gates and entering the passcode I gave him, I'm so turned on it's dangerous. The gates swing wide, and I get a clear look at the house. It's stunning, white and modern with high trees surrounding it for privacy.

The driver leaves my bags at the door at my request. The garage is open, revealing a black Lambo the owners left and a motorcycle. I bought the bike for Tyler as a gift. I hunted for ages for the vintage Triumph Bonneville. I'd considered having it fixed up before I gave it to him, but I knew he'd want to fix it himself. A way to blow off some steam.

Now it's pristine.

I trail a hand along the chrome and the leather seat in appreciation. The things my guy can do with his hands...

I open the door and step inside. My wedge sandals click on the marble as I steady my racing heart.

"That bike is hot," I call, pushing my sunglasses onto my head and scrunching a hand through the long, red hair I hope is still wavy after a day on the plane.

"If only I could find someone to take me on it."

The evidence of my arousal fills every syllable as I step out into the living room.

"And when I say, 'Take me'? I mean…"

I trail off, my throat tightening.

The man I love stands in the center of the vast room, seeming to fill the entire space with his presence.

Tyler Adams is breathtaking in profile. As gorgeous as ever in dark jeans that cling to his lean hips and strong legs, a white T-shirt that pulls across his chest and shoulders, revealing black ink that curls down his arm all the way to his fingers. His dark hair falls over his face, and when he turns to face me fully, he shoves it back.

The light from the floor-to-ceiling windows streams across his tan face, his cut jaw, and the firm mouth that tastes better than anything on this planet.

Tyler's heavy chocolate gaze locks on mine, holding me prisoner.

But it's his guilty expression that has me stunned.

And the fact that he's not alone.

End of Sample
To continue reading, be sure to pick up *A Love Song for Always* at your favorite retailer.

THANK YOU

If you read *A Love Song for Dreamers*...thank you. Thank you for trusting me with your time and your heart.

This series has taken me on a wild ride. It's undoubtedly the most raw, emotional story I've written. I'm so grateful for you participating in this with me. I hope Tyler and Annie stay with you for a long time to come. (And I'm not quite done with them yet...make sure you're on my VIP list to get updates on news from this world!)

My readers are the most amazing readers anywhere. You guys are positive, bold, enthusiastic, supportive, and amazing humans. I wouldn't write without you.

If you enjoyed *A Love Song for Dreamers*, I'd be beyond grateful if you could take two minutes to leave a quick review wherever you picked it up. Reviews are like gold to us authors - especially indies.

If you do leave a review, I'd love to hear about it so I can thank you personally. Here're the best ways to reach out:

www.facebook.com/piperlawsonbooks
www.instagram.com/piperlawsonbooks
piper@piperlawsonbooks.com

Thanks for being awesome, for inspiring me every day, and for helping make it possible for me to do something I love.

xoxo

Piper

BOOKS BY PIPER LAWSON

FOR A FULL LIST PLEASE GO TO

PIPERLAWSONBOOKS.COM/BOOKS

OFF-LIMITS SERIES

Turns out the beautiful man from the club is my new professor... But he wasn't when he kissed me.

Off-Limits is a forbidden age gap college romance series. Find out what happens when the beautiful man from the club is Olivia's hot new professor.

WICKED SERIES

Rockstars don't chase college students. But Jax Jamieson never followed the rules.

Wicked is a new adult rock star series full of nerdy girls, hot rock stars, pet skunks, and ensemble casts you'll want to be friends with forever.

RIVALS SERIES

At seventeen, I offered Tyler Adams my home, my life, my heart. He stole them all.

Rivals is an angsty new adult series. Fans of forbidden romance, enemies to lovers, friends to lovers, and rock star romance will love these books.

ENEMIES SERIES

I sold my soul to a man I hate. Now, he owns me.

Enemies is an enthralling, explosive romance about an American DJ and a British billionaire. If you like wealthy, royal alpha males, enemies to lovers, travel or sexy romance, this series is for you!

TRAVESTY SERIES

My best friend's brother grew up. Hot.

Travesty is a steamy romance series following best friends who start a fashion label from NYC to LA. It contains best friends brother, second chances, enemies to lovers, opposites attract and friends to lovers stories. If you like sexy, sassy romances, you'll love this series.

PLAY SERIES

I know what I want. It's not Max Donovan. To hell with his money, his gaming empire, and his joystick.

Play is an addictive series of standalone romances with slow burn tension, delicious banter, office romance and unforgettable characters. If you like smart, quirky, steamy enemies-to-lovers, contemporary romance, you'll love Play.

MODERN ROMANCE SERIES

When your rich, handsome best friend asks you to be his fake girlfriend? Say no.

Modern Romance is a smart, sexy series of contemporary romances following a set of female friends running a relationship marketing company in NYC. If you enjoy hot guys who treat their families like gold, fun antics, dirty talk, real characters, steamy scenes, badass heroines and smart banter, you'll love the Modern Romance series.

ABOUT THE AUTHOR

Piper Lawson is a WSJ and USA Today bestselling author of smart and steamy romance.

She writes women who follow their dreams, best friends who know your dirty secrets and love you anyway, and complex heroes you'll fall hard for.

Piper lives in Canada with her tall and brilliant husband. She's a sucker for dark eyes, dark coffee, and dark chocolate.

For a complete reading list, visit
www.piperlawsonbooks.com/books

Subscribe to Piper's VIP email list
www.piperlawsonbooks.com/subscribe

amazon.com/author/piperlawson

bookbub.com/authors/piper-lawson

instagram.com/piperlawsonbooks

facebook.com/piperlawsonbooks

goodreads.com/piperlawson

ACKNOWLEDGMENTS

First, thank YOU for picking up this book. I love that you trust me to entertain you.

This series happened because after I finished writing the Wicked trilogy, I couldn't get Tyler and Annie out of my head. At first I thought they needed a book, but once I got into their story, I realized it was more involved.

Some of the best love stories take time to tell—time in my life to get it on paper, but more importantly, time in the characters lives to grow up, to make mistakes and learn, and for everything to align so they can finally get their hard-won reward.

That's why these two get a trilogy. I hope their love, loss, and angst will tear you apart and make you whole again like it's done to me.

This series wouldn't have happened without the support of my awesome advance readers. Extra shoutout to Beth, Tammy and Michelle for doing an early read! You ladies rock.

Lori Jackson, Regina Wamba, and Kelley Hawthorne Jefferson, thank you for the perfect cover.

Becca Mysoor, thank you for your on-point advice. Cassie Robertson and Devon Burke, thank you for questioning, polishing, and catching all the little things.

Thank you Dani Sanchez for getting the word out about my stories. And Annette Brignac and Michelle Clay... I would not be able to get these books to the people who matter most without your help.

Thank you all from the bottom of my heart. The best part of author life is having YOU in it.

xoxo

Piper